Everything happened so fast. Shouted threats. Arrows. Gunshots.

Blue Feather lifted his spear, and with a shout that echoed against the buildings, he led the band back up Main Street, leaving enough dust behind to choke the breath out of those still standing in the street.

"What? Tell me!" Caroline screamed as Juliette appeared in the doorway. "Did someone die?"

All strength drained from Juliette's body as she snatched her precious Andrew from his sleeping place, her eyes widened from the deaths she'd just witnessed. As she cradled her son to her breast, she lifted a tear-stained face to her sister. "Oh, Caroline, what's to become of us?"

JOYCE LIVINGSTON is a real Kansas "lady" who lives in a little cabin that her husband built overlooking a lake. She is a proud grandmother who retired from television broadcasting, but she keeps very busy lecturing and teaching about quilting and sewing. She is also a part-time tour escort, which takes her to all kinds of fantastic places. She has had books and articles published on sewing, quilting, crafts, cooking, parenting, travel, personal color, and devotions—you name it. In 2000, she was voted Heartsong's favorite new author.

Books by Joyce Livingston

HEARTSONG PRESENTS

HP353—Ice Castle
HP382—The Bride Wore Boots
HP437—Northern Exposure
HP482—Hand Quilted with Love

Lucy's Quilt

Joyce Livingston

Heartsong Presents

This book is dedicated to Norman Arensdorf and his son, Jeff Arensdorf, the owners of Village Tours and Travel out of Wichita, Kansas, and Oklahoma City, Oklahoma. Since I am one of their part-time Tour Escorts, I get the privilege of escorting trips to all sorts of wonderful and exotic places, which I use as background settings for my stories. Thank you, Norman and Jeff! You're the greatest!

I'd also like to dedicate this book to our amazing Heartsong read-ers, especially those of you who take the time to write or e-mail me with your comments. This is my first historical novel, and I hope you enjoy it. As many of you know, I am a quilter, so it was only natural that I use a quilt as the focal point of *Lucy's Quilt*. I'd love to hear your reaction to my story.

A note from the author:
I love to hear from my readers! You may correspond with me by writing:

> **Joyce Livingston**
> **Author Relations**
> **PO Box 719**
> **Uhrichsville, OH 44683**

ISBN 1-58660-625-5

LUCY'S QUILT

All Scripture quotations, unless otherwise noted, are taken from the King James Version of the Bible.

The scene involving the Indians is loosely based on an incident that took place on June 2, 1859, in Council Grove, Kansas.

All of the characters and events in this book are fictitious. Any resemblance to actual persons, living or dead, or to actual events is purely coincidental.

Cover illustration by Lauraine Bush.

PRINTED IN THE U.S.A.

one

Dove City, Kansas, 1862

"Hello, Mrs. Martin." Stone Piper removed his hat as he entered the lobby of Dove City's only hotel. A large but crudely built structure on Main Street, it sat a few doors down from the general store. "Beautiful morning, isn't it?"

Juliette Baker Martin looked up from the ledger and smiled. "Yes, Mr. Piper, a beautiful morning indeed. Much too pretty to be working inside. What brings you to town on a day like this?"

The man fumbled around in his shirt pocket, pulled out a small white hanky, and held it out to her. "I—ah—wanted you—I thought you—"

She eyed him suspiciously as she lowered her pen, closed the ledger, and rose with a slightly guarded smile. She couldn't help but notice his weathered hand as she took the hanky from him. The finely woven threads seemed out of place balanced on his calloused fingers. "Wherever did you get such a lovely handkerchief?" Upon closer inspection, she noted the lace edge was a bit worn, but the intricate embroidery remained in perfect condition. His delicate gift and his gangly frame seemed incongruous.

"It belonged to Lucy, my wife," he stated simply.

His gaze met hers, and she thought it quite sad. Her heart went out to him. She knew she'd never be able to get over the grief of losing her own beloved husband. The pain was ever present. Certainly, Mr. Piper was feeling the same kind of pain.

"I've—I've been going through some of her things. Should've done it long ago. I—ah—thought you might like to have it. You being such a lady and all. . ." His voice trailed off

5

as if he had no idea how to finish his sentence.

She felt a sympathetic smile work at her lips as she unfolded the pristine cloth square and allowed her fingers to trace its delicate surface. "Lucy? What a pretty name."

Juliette knew he was at least fifteen years older than she. A friend of her father's, he was a widower and had two small sons living with his sister in Missouri. But according to her father, the man rarely talked about his past.

She smiled at the wrinkles in his shirt and the torn knee on his trousers. *He may be better off than most of us, but his clothing certainly doesn't show it*. It was obvious the man never shirked when it came to hard work and physical labor. The ladies in her sewing circle had said his spread was quite grand by Dove City standards, though she'd never seen it for herself. It wouldn't be proper for a woman of her status to visit a man's home unless accompanied by her parents.

Interested in Stone Piper or not, she had to admit her curiosity about Carson Creek Ranch. It sounded like the place of her dreams. A fine house, acres of timber, and the Neosho River flowing through it. No doubt, Mr. Piper had several fine horses. One day she was going to have a place like his, with her own fine horse to ride. Maybe two horses—one for her, another for Andrew. How or when she didn't know.

Looking back on her life, she wondered what would have happened if she hadn't married so young? Or had little Andrew when she was barely nineteen? What if she'd been single when she'd come west with her family instead of a widow with an infant to care for and support? Would her life have been so different? So hard?

"Ma'am?" His eyes lowered as his fingers moved nervously around the brim of his hat.

She felt a flush rise to her cheeks as she realized her mind had wandered far away from their conversation. "You—you were telling me about your wife? Lucy?"

"Yes, Lucy. She was as pretty as her name," he said proudly with a wistful smile that brought crinkles to his ruddy cheeks.

"I should've gone through her things long ago, but—" He swallowed hard. "But I just couldn't bring myself to do it."

She was embarrassed. How rude he must have thought her to let her mind wander like that when he spoke of such personal things.

"You—you must have loved her deeply," Juliette stammered as she refolded the handkerchief and returned it to the thoughtful man. Until now, she hadn't noticed how tall he was or how kind his deep-set blue eyes seemed. "Thank you, Mr. Piper, but—"

"Stone," he interjected quickly, then cleared his throat. "Call me Stone. Everyone does." He leaned against the counter with a friendly smile, the sadness she'd detected now replaced with warmth.

"Stone," she echoed nervously, feeling unworthy to be the recipient of such a personal gift. Her gaze locked with his as once more she extended the handkerchief toward him. "I can't accept something like this. Your daughters may someday want—"

"Don't have no daughters and don't rightly think there's any in my future. Only have sons." He held up a flattened palm between them. "Please, Mrs. Martin. Keep it. Lovely things should belong to a lovely lady."

Juliette felt another flush rush to her cheeks as she twisted the simple gold wedding band on her left hand. No one had called her *lovely* in a long time. Not since David—

"It'd be my pleasure, Ma'am, if you'd keep it."

When she met his earnest gaze, he was smiling convincingly. "Well—if you're sure you want me to have it. I hate to see you let something this lovely out of your family—"

He glanced quickly around the lobby, then leaned forward as if to share a secret. With a mischievous smile that seemed out of character for a man of his size, he whispered, "Oh, but I'm not intending to let it out of the family."

She frowned. "I don't understand, Mr. Pi—Stone."

To her surprise, he took her hand in his and gave it a slight squeeze. "I'm gonna ask your father, him being my friend, if it'd be alright for you and me to get married."

Juliette caught her breath sharply, dazed by his declaration. *Could he be teasing? Surely he isn't serious.* She had no idea how she should respond. "Ma–married?" she echoed as she stared up into eyes the color of the sky.

He gave her hand another squeeze, then turned to take his leave. "Not now, but soon. Don't let any other man claim you."

Smitten speechless, Juliette watched him go, then dropped onto the horsehair sofa near the hotel's fireplace, her knees suddenly unable to hold her weight, the dainty handkerchief still clutched in her hand. Had she heard Stone Piper right? Had he said he wanted to marry her? Whatever could he have meant by such a ridiculous remark? What an odd thing to say.

&

"When I get married, I'm going to marry a rich man," Caroline declared as she whirled about the room, holding baby Steven in her outstretched arms as the baby squealed with delight. "I'm going to have a big house with beautiful furniture, and—"

"While you're dreaming, little sister, dream up a rich man for me too," Juliette taunted with a grin that she knew made her dimples evident. If she dared put any stock in Mr. Piper's declaration, she wouldn't be needing any of her sister's dreams—not that she intended to take him up on his proposal. "I'll take a house too. Only much bigger. With lots of land and trees and a river running through it, and—"

Caroline laughed aloud, her chocolate brown eyes twinkling. "Whoa! Why don't you ask for the moon and the stars too? Come on, big sister, you'd better plan on settling for much less. You'll never find a man who can give you all of those things."

Juliette grabbed up her baby sister and rose quickly with a royal tilt of her chin. She whirled around the room in the same dizzying pattern as Caroline. "Maybe we can be neighbors and ride around in fine carriages, our babies on our laps, while other women do our work. That'd be mighty fine. Don't you agree?"

Caroline stopped laughing and appeared wounded. "Now

you're making fun of me."

Juliette grew serious as she stopped twirling and stood staring at her. "Not fun of you, Caroline. It's just that our dreams will most likely not become a reality. Life here on the prairie is hard for most folks. Very few came with an abundance of money in their pockets. We've been fortunate to live in this fine hotel. If our father hadn't been an educated man, he would've never gotten the job as hotel manager. We can thank the good Lord for that."

"I know," Caroline agreed thoughtfully. "But I'm keeping hold of my dreams. Someday—well, who knows what'll happen?"

Juliette glanced up the stairway. "Where's that sister of ours? We could use Molly's help with these tired babies."

"Molly's helping Mother change the beds. I told her to come down when she's finished, but you know how forgetful eight year olds can be. She's probably playing with her doll."

Juliette balanced her baby sister precariously on one hip and pulled aside the lace panel curtain covering the hotel's front window. It was nearly opaque with Kansas dust.

"I checked on Andrew. He's still asleep." Reuben leaned over the stair's railing, crunching on an apple.

"Thanks," Juliette said as she smiled at him. "Let me know when that son of mine wakes up."

Reuben nodded before heading back up the stairs, taking two steps at a time.

Caroline hoisted her crying sibling to her shoulder and moved behind Juliette for a better look. "What's all the shouting?"

Juliette cocked her head and listened. "I don't know, but something is wrong. I can sense it. Think you can take care of the twins by yourself for a few minutes? I'll go find out."

Caroline nodded. "I think what they both need is a good nap, but go ahead. I'll manage. Hopefully, Molly will come and help me."

Juliette gathered her skirts about her and hurried through the hotel lobby and onto the street, which had suddenly become as quiet as a watering pond on a still day in June. The few Dove City citizens who were out and about stood motionless, their gaze fixed on the end of Main Street. She hurried to join old Mrs. Pickford, jostling the woman's ribbon-trimmed bonnet in the process. "What is it, Bertha?" Juliette asked as she placed a hand on the elder woman's shoulder.

A worried frown twisted Bertha's wrinkled face as she answered with one word. "Kaws."

"The Kansa Indians?" Juliette asked quickly, remembering how her father had told her "Kaws" was the white man's term for the tribe. It wasn't unusual for Indians to be in the area. Whatever caused the woman's concern? She edged forward for a better look.

"Go back inside," a stern voice ordered somewhere behind her. She recognized it immediately without having to turn. It was her father. She knew better than to challenge his bidding, but she was concerned for the safety of her family. She continued to stare down Main Street at the approaching band of Indians, maybe one hundred strong, who were riding into town, all painted, feathered, and equipped for war. A chill of fear coursed through her body and caused a shudder. She'd never seen the Indians in war paint, and the sight frightened her.

"Now," her father ordered, and this time his tone was harsh as his long fingers dug into her shoulders. He spun her around. "Send Reuben out. We may need him."

She backed away slowly. Would her father never realize his eldest daughter had grown up? She was no longer a child but a woman. A mother with the responsibilities of an infant son, and part of that responsibility was to keep him safe. How could she keep him safe if she didn't know what was going on?

"Now, Child," he commanded, his voice unwavering as he stared her down. "You heard me."

She nodded before taking a final glance at the cloud of dust filtering up around the hooves of the horses that came to a sudden halt in front of the general store. Muttering to herself about the inequities of life, she hurried obediently back into the hotel.

"Kaws," she explained with a frown of concern as she entered, snatching up her baby sister. "I'm scared, Caroline, and I know Father is too. It looks like they're on the warpath."

Caroline's hand flew to her mouth, and she let out a loud gasp. "But, why?"

The lace curtains parted again as Juliette peered out, her nose pressed against the glass, Stella wrapped securely in her arms.

"Which one of you girls wants to change Andrew's diaper? He don't smell so good." Reuben held the giggling infant at arm's length and turned his head away.

Juliette wrinkled her nose, quickly placed her baby sister onto the pallet, and reached toward her tiny son, the offensive-smelling baby she loved more than life itself. In all the excitement, she'd nearly forgotten her father's request. "Reuben," she informed her younger brother quickly, "you'd better hurry outside. Father wants you. The Kaws are wearing war paint."

Reuben rushed toward the lobby door. "You girls stay in here where it's safe," he called back over his shoulder.

"You girls stay in here where it's safe," Juliette mimicked as she stooped to stretch her gurgling son out in his crib. "It's not fair, Caroline. I'm scared, and I want to know what's going on."

Her sister's eyes widened as she pointed a finger in Juliette's direction. "You'd better not let Father hear you talk like that."

"I'm nineteen years old," Juliette retorted with a lift of her chin and a shake of her head. "I should be able to go out onto the porch if I want to. I'm concerned about my son. How can I keep him safe if I don't even know what's happening out there?"

"As long as you're living under our father's roof, he'll expect you to do as he says." Caroline shifted Steven to her hip and moved to the window.

"It's not that I want to defy Father, Caroline. But I'm a mother now. It's my responsibility to keep my child safe, and I'm worried about you and mother and our brothers and sisters." Juliette clasped her fingers around her baby's thick ankles, lifted his plump legs, and placed a clean square of cloth under his bottom. "Someday, when I get married and have my own home, I'll be able to do as I please." As if on cue, Stone Piper's unexpected words flooded her mind. *I'm gonna ask your father, him being my friend, if it'd be alright for you and me to get married.*

Caroline turned from the window and placed Stella on the pallet beside Steven. "Another husband? What man would want to take on a woman with a six-month-old baby?"

"Plenty of men," Juliette responded quickly, tempted to tell Caroline of the morning's strange experience with the wealthy rancher. "I could've found one by now if I hadn't been so busy helping with this hotel and taking care of Andrew." She leaned toward the baby and planted a kiss on the tip of his tiny, pert nose. She loved caring for him and knew she was a good mother, but raising a baby in her father's home, in the midst of a large family with twin babies, was not an easy task. She'd much prefer to be on her own, but the meager salary she earned at her father's hotel ruled out that possibility.

Although the sisters couldn't see what was going on outside, they could hear it. The sound of nagging horses and agitated voices rose to peak level.

"I'm going out there just for a minute," Juliette announced as she handed her son to her sister. "Think you can keep an eye on the three of them? They're a pretty big handful. We need to know what's going on out there, and since no one has seen fit to come and tell us—"

Caroline reached out and clasped her hand around Juliette's wrist. "But Father said—"

Juliette pulled away and placed Andrew in the crib she'd bought to keep in the lobby so he could be near her when she worked. "I'm only going to have a quick look. Can I trust you to keep a close watch on my son?"

Caroline nodded. "You know you can."

Juliette moved through the lobby and out the door, doing a quick search of the area. Her attention went to the Indian's leader and Thomas Ward, whom she recognized immediately.

Mr. Ward was a bachelor and the owner of the general store. He and Blue Feather were having a heated exchange of words.

She pressed herself against the clapboard siding on the hotel front and moved a bit closer, clutching her skirts.

"You'd better get back inside, Juliette." It was Harrison Rogers, the young man who had accompanied the Baker family on their trip to Kansas from Ohio, and he was standing behind her.

"Mind your business, Harrison," she retorted with a cold stare and a shrug. Harrison was a nice young man and overly protective of her sometimes, even though they were nearly the same age. She was sure he was sweet on her, despite the fact that she was a widow with an infant to care for. He'd paid an inordinate amount of attention to her on the trail. But when and if she married again, it would be to a rich man—not to a mere boy seeking his fortune in this new land, no matter how nice he was.

"I heard your pa tell you to stay inside." His hand moved to the small of her back as he gave her a gentle shove in the direction of the hotel.

Her hands flew to her hips, and she stepped away from him. "If you tell Father, I'll—"

His hand caught her wrist, and his eyes twinkled mischievously as he leaned into her face. "You'll what? Kiss me?"

With a lifted brow and a coy smile—just coy enough to keep him obliged to her—she answered, "Kiss you? No, but I might be persuaded to do one of your chores for you. If you don't tattle on me. I need to see what's happening, Harrison. I have a son to worry about and need to keep him safe. You do understand, don't you?"

Harrison gave her a quick wink. "All right, just be careful and promise me you'll go back inside if any trouble starts."

She nodded. He was a nice boy but much too young, and he had nothing to offer her but himself and poverty, and she wanted neither. Maybe he'd be a good husband for Caroline, but not for her. "I promise."

Harrison gave her a grin of acceptance, then headed down to join some of the other boys his age who had gathered across the street from the confrontation.

Her heart clenched with sadness. How she wished David could have lived to see the Kansas prairie. He'd wanted so much to come to this territory. Too bad he'd never had that opportunity. Although at times she seemed ungrateful, she knew if it were not for her parents' willingness to take on the responsibility of a widowed daughter with a new baby, she would've been left behind with her father's sister. For that, she'd always be grateful. Life with her stern, maiden aunt would have been intolerable. If only there were some way she could repay her parents for all they'd done for her and her son.

As the voices of the Indian leader and Thomas Ward rose to an angry pitch, she strained to keep up with the words hastily being shouted by the interpreter.

"You sent for these two horses, which my boys stole from a Mexican trader," he told them as he translated the leader's words to the crowd. "You sent word that we must not only give up the horses, but we must turn over to you the two men who stole the horses, that your people might punish them." The leader's bony finger pointed menacingly toward the white man as he spoke.

Thomas Ward stood motionless and waited as he listened to what Mr. Claude Egan said as he acted as interpreter.

"The horses you can have, but the men you cannot have without a fight," Mr. Egan interpreted to the assembled group with exaggerated motions. "That's what he said."

"Who is he?" a woman asked a man standing beside her. "Is he the chief?"

He shrugged. "If you ask me, he's nuthin' but a troublemaker."

Juliette shuddered. It was common knowledge the Indians were not happy with the land settlement they'd been given by the government, and their discontent seemed to grow stronger with each passing day. Although the Indians were basically friendly, they would occasionally steal the settlers' horses and whatever else they could get their hands on if they thought they could do so without detection. The stealing of another man's horses was not taken lightly. A man could be hanged for such a crime.

Although she knew she should be heading back inside the hotel, she lingered long enough to see Thomas Ward's reaction to the Indian's statement. It appeared Mr. Ward was controlling himself as best he could. She'd heard he'd had many dealings with the Indians, and he seemed to know better than anyone how to handle them. But since the Indians had apparently come prepared to have a showdown, it appeared they had the advantage. Fear gripped her heart as she thought of her son, so young, so innocent, so undeserving of what might happen if an agreement couldn't be reached.

For some time, Mr. Ward stood silently, making no comment to Blue Feather's statement as the crowd waited for his response.

Juliette crossed her arms over her chest protectively and hunched her shoulders. *What if the Indians decide to attack?* There were so few men living in Dove City. Most of the men of the area were either farmers or ranchers and only came to town when they needed to make a purchase, have horses shod, or to attend church or a funeral. Some came to spend their time and hard-earned money in the noisy saloon.

She and the other onlookers stared in fear as Blue Feather and his followers began to taunt and insult the settlers.

Through the interpreter, she heard the Indian leader tell Thomas Ward and the others they had no business meddling with things that did not concern them. *Not concern us? When we're trying to live peaceably with the Kaw Indians? Of course, we're concerned,* she reasoned uneasily.

Mr. Ward continued to listen, his fists clenched at his sides as if he were struggling for control, as everyone watched for his reaction to the Indian's accusing words. He turned slowly to his clerk, who was cowering beside him, his face a sickly pallor, and loudly instructed him to bring two revolvers from his store.

Juliette and the others who remained watched spellbound, their hearts filled with fear as the clerk arrived with the guns and handed them to Thomas Ward one at a time. Slowly, he glanced around at the small crowd of citizens as if to assure them he was doing the right thing. His glance roved back to the Indians, now menacingly scattered about the area. Then back to Blue Feather. Everyone held their breath as he slowly lifted the two guns.

Boom! Boom! He fired two shots into the air as he glared at the leader, his eyes fixed on the man's painted face.

"Why'd he do that?" the woman asked as she buried her face in her companion's chest.

Juliette wondered the same thing. *What is his purpose? There's no way Mr. Ward can take on that large band of Indians with only two revolvers.*

"I'm sure it was to scare the Indians and show them he means business," the man explained as he stroked his wife's shoulder reassuringly. "But the main reason was to warn the settlers to get armed and be ready for whatever might occur."

Of course, Juliette thought as she searched the crowd for her father. *He did it to alert the settlers who aren't here. Word of the shots will spread rapidly, and men will drop whatever they're doing and come to help. I should have realized Mr. Ward would never do anything to jeopardize our lives.*

"Are they going to attack us?" the woman asked, her teary eyes filled with fright.

"Umm, I think they're only trying to outfox Ward," the man explained, never taking his gaze from the scene.

One of the warriors moved quickly to the front of the crowd, allowing his horse to trample those in his path. He lifted his bow in the air and let out a war cry that chilled Juliette's bones. It appeared he was taking it upon himself to lead his red brothers into battle, disregarding Blue Feather and his followers. As his horse whinnied and stood on its hind legs, the man ordered in his native tongue with Claude Egan translating, "Ward is shooting at us. Shoot him!"

With fear etched on their faces, the crowd of frantic men and women began rushing past Juliette as they struggled to escape the threat. She knew she should leave, but she was frozen to the spot, needing to know what happened. Once more, she pressed herself against the building, her eyes wide with terror, her heart thundering against her chest, her attention riveted on Thomas Ward. But to her amazement, he simply shrugged, turned his back on the aggressors, and moved into his store, shutting the door securely behind him.

Her glance flitted quickly toward where her father had been standing with Reuben, but they were nowhere in sight. Although she was relieved, she was also concerned. Her father knew almost nothing of the ways of the Indians or how they conducted their wars. He'd never been called upon during their time in Ohio to bear arms against anyone. He was a kind and gentle man with peaceful ways. Though he'd owned several guns, she'd never seen him use them. Yet, she knew if it became necessary, her father would take up arms and do all he could to protect his family. *Oh, Father, where are you?*

It was then she spotted them. Harrison had joined them, and the three had moved up directly behind where Mr. Ward had been standing. She was even more concerned for their safety. There was a fourth man she could barely make out in the swirling dust from the horses' hooves. It was Stone Piper, and she found herself concerned for his safety as well.

Some of the young bloods among the Indian band, those who seemed more restless than the others and eager to do battle, fired their guns. Charles Stark, the owner of the hotel her father managed, received a well-aimed arrow in the lower part of his neck.

Juliette gasped and watched in horror as the bleeding man twisted and fell to the ground. Never had she seen death happen so quickly. Her stomach lurched, and she thought she was going to be sick.

Another man she recognized as Mr. Morgan tried to cross the street. He was hit by one of the Indian's bullets, fell close to Mr. Stark, and lay motionless in a widening circle of his own blood.

Everything happened so fast. Shouted threats. Arrows. Gunshots. Screaming Indians. Horses rearing. People fleeing for their very lives. Never would she have believed this sort of confrontation possible in the quiet, friendly town they'd settled in only months before. She wanted to run to Mr. Morgan in the street to see if he was still alive, if he could be helped. But that was impossible. As she neared the safety of the hotel and pushed her way toward the doorway, she breathed a quick prayer of thanks. But as she was about to enter, Juliette turned to listen as she heard the terrified voice of the interpreter.

He was calling out loudly to the Indians in a vengeful tone that resonated through the emptying street as he pointed his long, slender finger at Blue Feather. "Your people have killed one man, maybe two. Get out of this town. Now!"

Blue Feather lifted his spear, and with a shout that echoed against the buildings, he led the band back up Main Street, leaving enough dust behind to choke the breath out of those still standing in the street.

"What? Tell me!" Caroline screamed as Juliette appeared in the doorway. "Did someone die?"

All strength drained from Juliette's body as she snatched her precious Andrew from his sleeping place, her eyes widened from the deaths she'd just witnessed. As she cradled her son to her breast, she lifted a tear-stained face to her sister. "Oh, Caroline, what's to become of us?"

two

Juliette and Caroline kept vigil at the window. Three long hours passed before her father and Reuben returned to the hotel lobby. Their faces told the story. Things did not look good.

"John, what happened to you? We were so worried!" Juliette's mother made her way to her husband and rested her head on his chest. "Juliette said Charles Stark was shot."

Her father sent a quick, accusing glare at Juliette, and she knew he would have preferred to tell his frail wife about Charles Stark's death himself.

"His death was quick. He didn't suffer." He cradled his wife's head in his big hand and stroked her cheek with the pad of his thumb. "We'll all miss him."

Her mother began to weep. "He has such a lovely family. How will they ever get along without him?"

"I don't know. Charles was a good man."

"What about the other man, Father?" Caroline asked.

"I don't know about the other man."

"Where have you been all this time? Surely you weren't out in the street when all this happened, were you?" her mother asked as she lifted her face and lovingly wiped a smear of dirt from his cheek. "The children and I were—"

"I know. I never meant to worry you. I should've sent word back with Juliette." He sent a frown Juliette's way, and she knew he'd seen her in the street after he'd ordered her back inside.

"Reuben and Harrison and I were with Deputy Piper and the other men. After the Indians left, we checked out the high ground south of Elm Creek, where the tribe had been camped."

"Did you find them?" Caroline asked. "Were they still wearing their war paint?"

"No, we didn't find them. We're assembling a council to determine what to do next. There weren't enough men in town to offer much resistance. I'm afraid the Indians knew it. We must thank God they left without causing further death or damage."

Juliette watched as her father once again forced a confident smile. "A call has gone out to those who live around here as well as the neighboring counties. We've asked all who can to hasten to Dove City as soon as possible." He swallowed hard, then added, "Prepared to fight."

Tears rolled down her mother's cheeks as she grasped his shirt. "Oh, John. No, not you. You're not a soldier. You must stay here at the hotel with us. We need you."

He lowered his head, his eyes focused on his wife. "The vote was unanimous. As men, we must protect our families."

Her mother drew in a deep breath and burst into tears as the rest of the family stood by silently, sickened by their father's words. "Oh, John. No. Not war."

He nodded as he once again began to stroke his wife's hair. "War seems inevitable. The sheriff's taking care of some trouble over at Heaton. But Deputy Piper is a good man, and the Indians seem to respect him. He'll lead us, and Egan is coming along as our interpreter. They're good, honest men, and both have had experience in dealing with the Indians. They don't want war any more than the rest of us. But, Mary, we have to make a stand."

Her grasp on his shirt tightened. "If you wait until tomorrow, more of the men can join you, and it won't be so dangerous. Please, John. Wait."

Lovingly, he pried her fingers away and pulled her into the shelter of his arms. "We can't wait, Mary," he said resolutely, his chin held high. "They might attack. Both Thomas Ward and Egan agree with Stone Piper."

Juliette stepped around the pallet and caught hold of her father's arm. "But why, Father? You said the Indians were gone."

"From what Deputy Piper said, we need to go out to scout their move. Perhaps they've only gone as far as Dry Bed Creek. That's too close for the comfort of the good people of Dove City."

With a heavy sigh, her mother leaned forward and took Stella from Caroline's arms.

Juliette watched as her father smiled, then chucked the baby under her chin as he continued, his face sobering. "The council believes if the Kaws are allowed to go unpunished for the outrage they've committed, there'll be no safety for any of us."

"You're going to follow them?" her mother asked as she hugged her baby, tears again trickling down her cheeks.

He didn't have to tell them. The answer was written on his weary face. "Pray for me, Mary. Please, pray for me like you've never prayed. If we've ever needed God's help, it's now."

&

"I've never been to war before," John Baker confided to Stone as they rode along. The heavy dust their horses kicked up dried their throats. "I'm not sure if I could shoot a man, even if he was a renegade Indian."

Stone shifted his weight in the well-worn saddle, his gaze intent on the trail stretching out before him. "Oh, you'd shoot him all right, John, if you had to. If it was your life or his or if he meant harm to one of your loved ones." He shielded his eyes and peered off in the distance toward a heavy clump of trees that could easily hide a warring band of Indians.

"Could you do it?"

Stone pushed his hat off his brow and wiped the sweat from his forehead. "Only if I had to." A bird sounded a mournful cry, and both men turned in its direction, listening carefully before resuming their conversation. They feared the whistle might not be a bird's, but an Indian's. A pair of rabbits leaped from their hiding place in the tall grass and scurried across the trail in front of them. "I pray to God I won't be faced with that decision."

They rode along in silence, the drumming of forty sets of

horses' hooves beating down the prairie grasses the only sound. None of the riders seemed to have much to say as each kept his eyes trained dead ahead toward Dry Bed Creek, which lay off in the distance beyond the dense grove of trees.

Stone took in a deep breath of the warm morning air. "Those redskins could be watching us right now."

"You know the Indians better than I do." John shrugged and tightened the grip on his reins.

He didn't want to say anything to John, but he was concerned about the womenfolk and children they'd left behind in Dove City. Undoubtedly, the Indians knew their number and could, if they were of a mind to, send some braves back into town to— He didn't even want to think what they might do. "Long enough to know you can't trust most of these Indians. I can't say that I blame them much."

"Oh?" John's brows rose in question.

"Not the way the government handled the land acquisitions. The Indians think they got a raw deal. Sometimes I'm inclined to agree with them."

John frowned. "But does that give them the right to take what they want? Even kill?"

Stone shook his head and spat on the ground. "Course not. But those Kaws didn't want to come here in the first place. They'd have rather stayed near Topeka, along the Kansas River. It was the government's idea to bring them to Dove City, even promised the Indians the choice land along the upper valley of the Neosho River, where the tall timber grows."

"You'd have thought they'd have been happy with that," John reasoned aloud. "Good land and abundant water. What more could they ask?"

"Oh, that's what they were promised but not what they got. Too many problems with some messed-up survey, and a lot of the settlers homesteaded on Indian lands by mistake." Stone ordered a halt. The troop of inexperienced would-be soldiers stopped abruptly. Everyone peered off into the distance at the approaching band of riders.

Stone glanced over his shoulder as his hand moved instinctively to the holster mounted at his side. "Kaws. Keep your peace, men," he called out to his troops. "We don't want to anger them."

Forty men sat straddling their horses as fear shone in forty sets of eyes.

The Indians began to circle them, posting themselves to the best advantage—tantalizing the men, goading them, and beckoning them to come on and fight.

"I'd like to shoot that miserable—" one of the riders positioned next to Stone told him under his breath just loud enough for those closest to him to hear.

Stone remained motionless but cautioned, "Don't even think it. They want us to start something. These Indians have been trained from boyhood to fight. We wouldn't stand a chance. One move from us, and it's all over. Keep your peace, Man. Keep your peace."

The man settled himself back into his saddle and said nothing more. Apparently Stone's message had brought him to his senses.

"Are we going to just sit here and wait for them to kill us?" John asked nervously, his eyes trained on the circling renegades.

Stone whispered to his interpreter, "Egan, I think we'd better send someone out to talk to the Indians and try to reason with them to avert further bloodshed. Looks to me like we're at their mercy."

Mr. Egan listened intently. "I agree with you. Getting them stirred up won't help anything. Perhaps talking will. Let me have a try. I'll ask for a peaceful settlement of this dispute and let them know that a war between our two factions will mean loss to both sides. I'll tell them, if that happens, the government will certainly step in and take measures of its own."

Stone nodded. "Do it."

Egan slowly rode toward the Indian who appeared to be in charge, and the two talked in hushed tones.

"It's not working. They're not backing off," John muttered

as his fingers clutched the reins.

"True. But they're not making any warlike moves either," Stone reminded him. "That's a good sign. Let's hope our man can convince them nothing good can come to them by attacking us."

Taking his gaze off the pair for only a second, Stone singled out two of the younger men. "Ride back to Dove City as quickly as your horses can carry you, and tell the others of what's happening. Tell them we need reinforcements as soon as possible. Our negotiations here seem to be at a standstill."

Without a questioning word, the two men rode off.

"All we can do is wait," Stone whispered. "Wait and pray."

❧

"I wish I were there." Juliette's fist banged against the counter. "I hate being left behind and not knowing what's happening, especially when it could be affecting our very lives."

"But you're a woman. You know what they could do to you—"

"Not if I had my gun," Juliette responded resolutely with narrowed eyes and a defiant tilt of her chin. "I'd do whatever was necessary to protect my son and the rest of my family."

"Your gun? You don't have a gun," her sister reminded her. "You've never even shot a gun, have you?"

Someone stormed into the hotel and announced the Kaw mission had been opened as a temporary shelter for those families waiting for their husbands and fathers to return.

"Now, what were you saying about having a gun?" Caroline asked as many of the hotel's overflow of occupants headed out the door.

"I don't have a gun, Caroline. If I were a boy, I'd have a gun."

Caroline shook her head.

❧

The troop of forty men grew to nearly two hundred as groups of armed men on horseback rode out from Dove City and Clacker County to join the others. With their addition, confidence grew among the settlers.

"I think we should try to talk to them again, Egan," Stone

advised as he made his way up to their interpreter's side.

"I agree." Egan brought his horse closer to Stone's and tugged on the reins. "I'm hopeful I can get through to them. I know the Indians personally. I've had their children in school. Surely they know we're a peaceful people, and we're trying to avoid any more bloodshed."

Stone put a hand on the man's shoulder. "You do know the risk, Egan? They could kill you just like that." He snapped his fingers for emphasis. "Since we're still outnumbered, we'd be hard-pressed to do much about it. But I have faith in you. I know those Indians look up to you. I think you're the only one who can negotiate with them effectively."

Egan pulled his hat lower on his brow. "I'll do my best."

There was a space of about two hundred yards between where the white men halted and where the Kansa Indians had taken up their position. Stone knew, from the Indians' vantage point, they could see more reinforcements arriving on the settlers' side. He hoped they would be dissuaded from taking any action they'd all regret later. *God, I know I have no right to ask this, but if You hear me, make them listen to reason. We don't want war.*

The settlers formed a consolidated line as Egan made his move to speak to Blue Feather a second time. Each man stood ready to advance at the first indication of treachery. Mr. Egan was met by the chief, and the two men talked in low tones.

The entire troop watched with heightened interest as the chief called together his key men into a guarded circle, where they spoke. He then relayed their decision to Egan, who hurried back to Stone and the others.

"They'll surrender the Indian who shot Morgan but not the one who shot Stark. They say they are not sure which man wounded him."

"Do you believe him?" Stone asked.

"No," came Egan's quick reply. "I think what they're doing is trying to save their young brave. I'm sure he's the one who shot Stark, but he serves on the council and appears to be of great value to the tribe."

Stone stroked his beard thoughtfully. "I think we're all in agreement here, Mr. Egan. Tell the chief we're not interested in such an arrangement. We'll accept nothing short of a surrender of the two Indians."

A hush fell over both the Indians and settlers as Egan spoke with Blue Feather. Within minutes, he was back with a new offer. "They say they'll pay us eight hundred dollars and forty ponies as satisfaction for the shooting of Stark, but I said no."

"And well you should have," Stone stated in quick response as his narrowed eyes surveyed the vast number of horses and riders who had gathered on his side. His troops now numbered over four hundre´, and he was sure more were on their way. "We will take nothing less than the surrender of those two Indians."

Dread ran through the settlers as the young brave suddenly appeared before them, armed and prepared to fight, still wearing his war paint. As he spiraled his arm into the air and shouted to the others, Mr. Egan interpreted in a high-fevered pitch so all could hear. "He says, since they've decided to surrender him, thereby sanctioning his death, he'll sell his life as dearly as possible. If necessary, he'll kill his own chief, then the white man who demanded his surrender!"

Nodding, Stone signaled for his men to make ready but to hold their fire.

Although the brave's fiery speech seemed to stir up the other young braves, it appeared to have no obvious effect on the tribal elders, who held their silence. Yet, they seemed hesitant to give the man up.

Stone's hand moved to grip the saddle horn. He watched as Mr. Egan squared his shoulders and, once again, spoke to Blue Feather.

"Now what?" John asked, his penetrating look trained on the Indian chief and Egan.

Stone's gaze hardened. "Knowing Egan, I'm sure he's still

trying to work something out. All we can do now is wait."

The settlers watched impatiently, still hoping for a resolution to the volatile situation. In a matter of minutes, Mr. Egan returned. "Their offer has increased to one thousand dollars and the horses." He removed his hat and slapped it against his leg, then shook his head wearily. "I told them they have committed an outrage upon the settlers and shed the blood of two innocent people. Unless both are given up, our men are determined to fight."

Hating to say the words but knowing they had to be said, Stone nodded. "You were right to tell them that. As much as we hate war, we are prepared to do battle if it becomes necessary. I'm sure they understand our position. What else did you tell them?"

"Sir, I told them if both Indians are not surrendered by the time I return to my people and count to twenty, the consequences rest upon them. I told them when I set my stick upon the ground, they will know I have finished my count."

Stone saluted Claude Egan and instructed, "Then go, Mr. Egan. Take your stick and count. When you have finished counting, set it upon the ground as you've said. We're ready."

"Lord, help us. They're not conceding," John declared loudly.

Stone could sense the fear in his voice and was sure John was preparing to die. He reached across and clamped his hand around his friend's arm. "Have faith. It's not over yet. But if we must do battle, let me lead the way. You're important to your family. Mine cares nothing about me."

John shook his head with a grateful smile. "Thanks, Stone. But I'll do my part in defending our families and friends. If you make it and I don't—" He hesitated and gulped. "Promise you'll tell my family I love them and I died to keep them safe."

Stone tightened his grip on the man's arm. "I will, John. I promise; but we're both going to make it, do you hear?"

All eyes focused on the courageous mediator as he slowly

walked to the halfway mark, then loudly counted to twenty before placing the stick on the ground.

The silence was deafening. Even the birds stopped their singing as three hundred Indians and at least five hundred settlers sat on their horses, anticipating each other's next move.

Suddenly, in a loud, clear voice, the chief yelled out, "We're ready to give up the two guilty men."

A sigh of relief washed across the line as Mr. Egan quickly interpreted the Indian's words. Men smiled at one another and relaxed their grips on their weapons a bit.

"God has answered our prayer, Stone," John cried out as he heard the words of the chief. "We aren't going to have to fight."

Stone leaned forward on his horse and stroked the animal's mane. "I know, John. I know."

Minutes later, the guilty pair were brought forth, bound, and delivered to Deputy Piper.

"What happens now?" John asked Stone.

"They'll be put on their horses and ride back to town behind us. Probably go to trial."

"And death?"

Stone nodded. "Yes. Death."

❧

"Any word yet?" Juliette asked as she picked up little Steven and hugged him. "It's been hours since our father left. I pray to God he's all right."

Caroline led her mother to the worn sofa and asked two ladies to scoot over so she could sit down between them.

"Having those twins on the trail is what ruined her health," Juliette told her sister, taking her aside so no one else could hear. "Father should never have allowed her to come to Kansas with us. The trip was too hard for her. He should've left her behind and gone back for her later."

Caroline backed off in surprise, cupping her hand to her mouth before replying. "Left her behind? You know she'd never stand for that. Father and Mother have rarely been separated since the day of their wedding."

"If you ask me, I think the idea of bringing a woman with child on such a long journey was stupid," Juliette said in a whisper as she brushed the dust from her skirt and straightened her bodice. "Especially one in bad health."

"But he didn't ask you," Caroline reminded her in a snit. "Look at you. Andrew was born not long before we left Ohio. Do you think Father should have left you behind?"

"Of course not," Juliette answered indignantly, finding it hard to keep her voice down. "That's different. I'm only thinking of our mother, Caroline. It makes me sad to see her feeling so poorly all the time."

One of the ladies, an elderly woman named Ethel Benningfield, moved from the sofa and made her way toward them. Her gaze concentrated on Juliette. "Dear," she began with a friendly smile, "please don't talk that way about your parents. I'm sure if your father had any doubt about bringing your mother along, he wouldn't have made the trip at all."

Surprised by the woman's words, Juliette simply stared at her.

"I know you mean well, but one should never criticize her parents' actions—especially someone with parents like yours. You're lucky to have them both with you. I lost mine in a fire when I was only nine."

"I–I'm so sorry," Juliette stammered, thinking back over what she'd said. "That must have been very difficult for you."

The woman touched Juliette's wrist as she smiled up into her eyes. "You have no idea how difficult. God has given you girls wonderful, godly parents. Love them while you still have them, and support them in everything they do. They always have your best interests at heart." With that, the woman turned and walked away.

"I didn't think anyone could hear us," Juliette whispered to Caroline. "But she's right. I should never have criticized Father for bringing Mother along. My mouth is always getting me in trouble."

One of the wives who'd moved outside earlier burst into the

lobby. "They're coming! There's a terrible cloud of dust on the horizon."

Everyone hurried outside, hoping to see their loved ones returning. Juliette and Caroline followed close behind, carrying their siblings.

"Father has to be all right," Caroline said as she shielded her eyes from the afternoon sun. "It would kill Mother if anything happened to him."

"When I marry again, I'm going to be strong for my husband. I'm going to ride by his side as an equal. I won't let him leave me behind."

"Ha," her sister retorted. "You're just looking for trouble, Juliette. If Father heard you talk—"

"Well, I am," she broke in. "My husband will be proud to have a strong woman for a wife."

Caroline laughed aloud. "What husband? I haven't seen any men pursuing you lately, Mrs. Martin—rich or poor."

Juliette tucked an errant curl behind her ear. "That's because you haven't noticed. Only today," she bragged, "a man told me he was going to marry me."

"Who?"

Now she had her sister's full attention. "I'm not telling."

Caroline smirked. "Because you've made him up, that's why."

Juliette lifted her chin arrogantly. "Did not. He's a real man and a handsome one too, I might add. And he has a beard."

Her sister moved closer. "Who, Juliette? Who? If he was real, you'd tell me his name."

"I'm not telling. It's our secret—his and mine."

Caroline cocked her head and looked dubious. "You wouldn't lie to me, would you?"

"Of course not. I don't lie. I can't stand people who lie."

"Then tell me who he is."

"Only when we're ready to announce our engagement."

Caroline's eyes grew bright with anticipation. "You mean you've accepted?"

Juliette thought for a minute. As usual, she'd said more

than she'd intended. It was a nasty habit of hers, making more of something than it really was. Well, she'd backed herself into a corner, and her sister was waiting for an answer. She drew a deep breath, and deciding how much she could say without telling one of those lies she hated so much, she looked directly into her sister's eyes. "Not yet. I'm still thinking about it."

three

Stone tugged his hat low on his brow with a relieved grin as he and John rode ahead of his men. "Well, things certainly look better now than they did this morning."

The look on John's face grew serious. "Better in some ways. Worse in others."

Stone's brow creased. "Worse? I don't understand."

"I may not have a job."

"Oh?" Stone responded. "Why'd you say that?"

John pulled off his hat and swatted at the sweat bee buzzing around his face. "Charles Stark owned the hotel. With him gone now, I have no idea what his family will do with it. His wife is too old to run the place, and his children have no interest in it. That's why he hired me. If I lose my job at the hotel, we won't even have a roof over our heads."

"You and your family can stay with me until you line something up. You're always welcome in my home. I've got plenty of room, even for your large family."

"And three squalling infants?"

Stone grinned. "Even them."

The group rode victoriously into town and stopped in front of the general store, filling the street to overflowing with relieved faces and renewed spirits. Women and children moved in to hug their husbands, fathers, and brothers and for a better look at the two Indian braves tied onto their horses.

"Hang them!" a voice shouted from the back of the crowd. "They killed Charley and Mr. Morgan. They deserve to die!"

The crowd took up the chant. "Hang them. Hang them."

Thomas Ward stepped out from his store and lifted his hand for silence. "Without a trial? You want these men hanged?"

"They didn't give Charley Stark a trial, and he hadn't done

32

nothing to them," one of the older men called out as he shook a fist in the air. "I say hang them. Here and now."

"He's right," called out another. "Hang them."

Again the crowd took up the chant. "Hang them. Hang them."

Thomas Ward raised his arms in defeat as he called out loudly, "Then let their blood be on your hands!"

A pair of nooses were readied at an old cottonwood tree next to the bridge. The crowd, chanting and shouting, followed as the two men's horses were led to the spot.

In final protest, Thomas Ward stepped up onto a stump where all could see him and shouted to the crowd, "Should these men be hanged without a court? Or an attorney? Or without a judge to hear their case? Is that what you say?"

"There is no case," Mr. Stark's widow shouted. "They killed my husband, a good man. Now, they deserve to die." Several of the younger men led the violators' horses beneath the nooses and slipped the loops over the Indians' heads as the shouts of the crowd spurred them on. Thomas Ward scanned the crowd again. "These men shed the blood of two white men who did them no injury, and justice demands they should suffer death. Is that what ye say?"

"Yes. Yes. Yes!" came the unanimous cry from the people.

Mr. Ward raised a fist into the air. "Then, so be it."

A hush of anticipation fell over the assembled throng. Mothers covered the eyes of impressionable children, and husbands wrapped their arms about sensitive wives. The certainty of impending death hung heavily in the air as every adult focused on the men whose demise was only seconds away.

Juliette felt a strong arm about her shoulders. It was Stone. At that moment, she needed the strength of a good man. About to witness her first hanging, the fiery independence she normally felt had been replaced with little girl fear. As she felt his arms tighten around her, she leaned into him for support.

The robust crowd, who had earlier been so vocal, remained silent as they beheld death in the making. The same men who'd placed the nooses about the Indians' necks slapped the rumps of the Kaws' mounts. They took off in a run, leaving the braves dangling from the tree at the end of their ropes.

Life was a precious commodity. Everyone present had just been witness to the end of two young braves' existence. Their lives had been traded for the lives of Charles Stark and Mr. Morgan. Justice had been done.

"This is a sad day for Dove City," Stone whispered in Juliette's ear. "A sad day, indeed. One death is avenged with another, and the chain goes on. Where, oh where, will it all end?"

∾

The day dawned gray, cool, and cloudy. It was as though nature itself mourned for the men who had died so needlessly at the Indians' hands.

Nearly all of Dove City's citizens attended the funeral of Charles Stark.

Juliette clutched Andrew tightly and tried not to cry as she agonized over the grief on Charles Stark's widow's and children's faces. Just being there among Mr. Stark's family and friends made her think of David and his funeral only a few short months before. "Your daddy loved you," she whispered as Andrew's pudgy fingers played at her lips.

"Anyone sitting here?"

Taken aback, she looked up into the clear blue eyes of her father's friend. Although she would have preferred the seat remain vacant, she shook her head. "No, no one."

Stone sat down beside her. "Then, if it's all right with you, I'll be taking this seat."

He balanced his hat on one knee and whispered softly as he leaned toward her ever so slightly, "He was a good man."

"I know."

"Too bad about his death."

"Yes, it is." Filled with sudden, unexpected emotion, Juliette pulled a hanky from her bag and dabbed at her eyes.

"Should've been me."

She turned quickly and lifted her face to his. "What? What did you say?"

He swallowed hard as deep furrows formed on his forehead. "Been better if it'd been me instead of Stark."

Her eyes grew wide. Surely she'd misunderstood. "Why would you ever say such a thing?"

He let out a deep sigh. "Stark has people who'll miss him. No one would miss me."

Juliette found herself without words and simply stared at the man seated beside her.

"Seems God always takes the best for Himself and leaves the rest of us to mourn."

Before she could respond, Pastor Tyson stepped up and the service began. Men blinked and women wept as the Scripture was read and the pastor spoke. After his message, several folks, including Stone and her father, said kind words about the man they'd come to bury. After that, Emma Fritz sang "Amazing Grace." There was not a dry eye in the huge room. By the time the final words were spoken, a heavy rain began to fall and lightning split the sky.

"You girls get the buggy and take your mother on home," John Baker told his daughters. "I'm afraid this has been too much for her."

"Can't Caroline and Molly take her, Father? I want to go on to the cemetery," Juliette explained as she stepped away from him. It was as though going to the cemetery would put an end to her grieving for David. She'd been so numb at his funeral, she could barely remember a word that had been said. Now, despite the tumultuous storm outside, she felt drawn to Lone Tree Cemetery. Perhaps there she could say the good-bye she felt she'd never said to David and have the peace she so desperately sought.

"I don't think it's a good—"

"I need to go, Father," Juliette interrupted with deep conviction. "Please."

"Then let Caroline take the baby back with her," her father advised as he reached for Andrew.

"No." Juliette turned away, clutching her baby tightly. "I

want him there with me. He needs to be there when I—"

Her father reached for Andrew again. "He's much too heavy for you to carry for so long. Let me have him."

She twisted to one side, avoiding his grasp. "Don't you see, Father? Andrew is all I have left of David. I want him near me. I'm his mother. I know he's just a baby, but—"

She felt a strong hand on her shoulder. "I'll help her with the baby, John. Don't worry about her. I'll see she gets home all right."

The kindness in Stone Piper's eyes and his consideration of her feelings touched her deeply. Was he the only one who understood the ache in her heart?

He instructed her to wait until he could bring the buggy around to the front. Juliette watched as he strode out the door and wondered at his strange comment that it should have been him who died, instead. That no one would miss him. *Whatever would cause a good man like Stone Piper to make such a foolish statement?* He seemed to have a habit of making comments she didn't understand.

When Stone returned, he bolted off the seat and up the steps with an open umbrella. Taking Andrew in one arm, he escorted Juliette to his buggy.

The rain had lessened somewhat by the time he halted his team. He offered his hand to help her down, and they joined the other mourners around the grave. She felt faint as her eyes fixed on the gaping hole and the mound of dirt surrounding it. She barely remembered David's funeral. Had there been a mound of dirt like that beside his grave? Had it been sunny? Or rainy? She couldn't remember. All she could remember was that her beloved husband left her that day, put into the ground like a faded flower.

"Maybe I'd best take you on home, Juliette. Perhaps your father was right," Stone whispered as his grip tightened about her.

She managed to rein in her emotions and, with a quaver in her voice she hoped went undetected, answered, "No, I want to stay. I owe it to the Stark family."

"Death is never easy for those left behind."

His words cut through her being. They both knew the meaning of those words. Each had lost their spouse, just like the Widow Stark. "No," she muttered softly as her eyes filled with tears. "It's never easy."

By the time the graveside service ended and mourners were making their way toward their wagons, the rain had stopped and the clouds were dissipating.

When they arrived at the hotel, Stone jumped down from his seat, hurried around to Juliette's side, and took the sleeping infant from her arms. He handed him to Caroline, who'd come out of the hotel to greet them. Instead of offering a hand as he'd done at the cemetery, he reached up and lifted Juliette down from the seat. For a brief moment, their eyes met. To her surprise, Juliette felt as though she'd known this man all her life, and she knew she could trust him. He'd never do her any harm.

"Thank you, Mr. Piper," she said sweetly, fully appreciating the efforts he'd made on her behalf.

"Stone."

Despite the ruddy complexion on his suntanned face, she caught a glimpse of a slight blush as he fingered the brim of his hat.

"Remember? You're supposed to call me Stone."

"Of course, Stone. Thank you."

"Glad you like the hanky, Ma'am."

"Hanky?"

He reached up to the seat where she'd just ridden and picked up the soggy hanky she'd used to dab at her swollen eyes. The one he'd given her the day he'd said he was going to marry her. The one that had belonged to his wife.

"Oh," she said, embarrassed that she hadn't remembered she'd brought it. "Yes, I do like it. I carry it often. Thank you."

"I'm glad. I wanted you to have it."

"I'm honored you gave it to me."

He moved away, nearly getting his big feet tangled in the process. "My pleasure, Ma'am."

On impulse, Juliette stood on her tiptoe and gently brushed a kiss across his cheek.

"Ah—thank you," he stammered as he continued to back away. "Gi–give my best to your family. I hope your mother gets to feeling better real soon. Guess I'll be going now."

Juliette smiled as she watched him climb onto the buggy and ride off down the muddy street. *What a nice man Stone Piper is. What a shame his wife died so young. He must've been a fine husband.*

She laughed aloud as she remembered his comment about marrying her. *Surely he didn't mean what he said.*

❧

"Good morning, Mrs. Stark. What a nice surprise." Juliette rushed to assist the pale widow as she entered The Great Plains Inn. "I've been meaning to call on you—"

The kindly lady lowered herself onto the horsehair sofa with great effort. "You needn't explain, Dear. I know how hard it is to call on someone who's lost a loved one. It's difficult to find the right words. As a widow, you probably understand more than most what I'm going through."

Juliette knelt at her side and wrapped her arms about the trembling woman. "I do know, Mrs. Stark. If it hadn't been for my wonderful family, I'd never have made it. I'm sure your family is there for you too."

The woman nodded. "Yes, my daughters have been with me constantly since Charles—" She gulped uneasily.

"I'm sure they'll continue to take good care of you," Juliette assured her confidently. "Families take care of their own."

"They try to—"

"I'll tell Mother you're here. I know she'll want to see you," Juliette offered, rising. She sensed Mrs. Stark's need to talk but felt inadequate to deal with the subject of Mr. Stark's death.

The woman quickly grasped her wrist. "No, Juliette. It's not your mother I've come to see. It's your father."

"Father? Really?"

"Yes, I need to speak with him. It's very important."

"I'm here, Mrs. Stark." Her father stepped into the lobby with a gentle smile toward the woman. "I've been expecting to hear from you. I'm assuming this is about the hotel. Am I correct?"

"I'm sorry, John. I wish there was some other way, but I must sell the hotel as quickly as I can." Her face brightened a bit. "Perhaps you could buy it."

Father shook his head. "I could try to get a loan, but the bank requires collateral. I have none."

"I hope you'll be able to raise the money, John. If the bank wants a reference, I'll be happy to tell them what a wonderful manager you've been." She appeared thoughtful. "Or perhaps someone else would give you a loan. One of the local ranchers, maybe?"

"Hmm, I can't really think of anyone with that kind of money who would part with it without adequate collateral."

"Just a thought." Mrs. Stark adjusted her hat and slowly walked toward the door. "Believe me, this is the only way."

He nodded with a forced smile. "I'm sure it is. I'll do what I can."

"I'll wait to hear from you before I take any further steps. Good day, John. I do hope Mary begins to feel better soon. Please convey my good wishes to her."

"I will, and thank you for coming. Good day."

Juliette found it hard to even say good-bye to the woman. She watched as her father lowered himself onto the sofa. "Father? Are you all right?"

Slowly, he lifted his worried face, his misty-eyed gaze pinned on her. "For the first time in my life, I feel totally helpless; but your mother can't know, Juliette. I'm depending on you. We can't let her discover the hopelessness of our situation. Tomorrow I'll go to the banker, and if I don't get any help there, I'll begin looking for another job. I have no experience in farming or ranching, but I'm able-bodied and I can learn. I'm just not sure anyone will want to take the time to teach me."

"You've never let this family down, Father. If you lose the hotel, Caroline and Reuben and I will find other jobs elsewhere. We may not make much, but whatever we earn will help until you find employment."

He lifted his face proudly, his shoulders now squared. "My children work to support my family? Never. Helping here at the hotel is quite enough."

"But, Father—"

"No. I won't hear of it. The day John Baker's children have to support his family will be his last day on earth. Do you hear me, Juliette? I'll die first."

Shocked by his statement, she gasped. She'd never heard such words from her normally soft-spoken, peaceful father. "But, if you can't get—"

"If I can't get the loan, I'll feed swine, dig wells, clean stables—any job I can get. But I won't lean on my children."

"But—"

John's fingers circled her wrist, and she winced. "That's quite enough, Juliette. Now, go check on Andrew while I see to your mother. I don't want to hear another word of such foolishness."

She pulled away from his grasp, rubbing at the place. "Yes, Father. I'm sorry. I never meant it as an insult. You've been a wonderful father to me and treated me far better than I deserve. I just wanted to help ease the burden around here. I owe it to you."

"You owe me nothing but respect, Daughter, and I have to earn that." John's face softened as he took Juliette's wrist and gently stroked the area with the pad of his thumb. "I'm sorry, Honey. I didn't mean to be so rough. Taking care of my own flesh and blood is important me. Trust me, all right?"

Juliette watched her father slowly climb the stairs as if each step were cumbersome. His normally straight body was hunched over, and she wanted to cry.

૨

"Good morning, John. What are you doing at the bank so early?"

John turned to see Stone tying his horse's reins to the railing. "Didn't expect to see you in town."

"It's America's fault. That housekeeper of mine had a long list of supplies, and Moses couldn't come. I told her I'd ride in, take care of some business, and pick up her needs." He walked up to John and gave him a friendly slap on the back. "You don't look so good. What's wrong?"

John shook his head. "Had some trouble sleeping last night, that's all. Mary isn't doing very well. I'm worried about her."

"She has looked pale lately. I just thought she'd overdone. Taking care of those twins has got to be hard work."

"Those two are a handful all right, but Juliette and Caroline are a big help. And Molly too. But I'm afraid it's more than overdoing. She hasn't been well since we left Ohio. I guess we need to have Doc take a look at her."

"Probably a good idea. Well, I'd best be tending to my chores. I sure don't want to upset America by making her wait on her flour and sugar." Stone added with a grin, "You know how women can be when they're out of supplies. Good cooks are hard to find. I have to pamper that woman."

"As if she'd ever leave you. You brought her all the way from Kentucky, and you treat her like a queen—probably better than most men treat their wives. But you're lucky to have America and Moses. Those two are as loyal as they come."

Stone gave his friend a grin and a tip of his hat. "That they are. See you later."

૨

Stone finished his shopping and was putting the supplies in the wagon when the door to the bank opened. John appeared, his face drained of all color.

"John? What's wrong?"

John leaned his back against the stone building, his shoulders hunched, his chin resting on his chest.

Stone hurried to him. "What is it? Are you sick?"

John didn't answer. He just stared at his feet in silence.

"Speak to me. Do I need to go get Doc?"

"I'm—fine," a weak voice responded.

"Let me walk you to the hotel," Stone offered as he forced his arm around John's shoulders.

"No. Not the hotel. Not now." This time John's voice was firm. "I can't face my family right now."

"All right. Then let me help you into my wagon, and we'll go somewhere we can talk."

Stone led him to the wagon and assisted him onto the seat, then drove out of town, reining up under a large sycamore tree. "Gonna tell me about it?"

John let out a moan as his hands covered his face. "They said no, Stone. I don't know what I'm going to do."

"Who said no? What are you talking about?"

"The bank. They refused to give me a loan. Mrs. Stark is going to sell the hotel. She thought I'd be the logical person to buy it. I explained I had very little money and no collateral, but she suggested I go to the bank for a loan."

"That's what you were doing when I saw you there earlier?"

John nodded.

"They turned you down?" Stone's eyes widened. "Just like that? Knowing the fine way you've managed the hotel?"

"Didn't seem to matter to them. Collateral—that's what they want, and I don't have any." With a mocking laugh, John pulled out his empty pockets.

"So, what are you going to do?"

"What *can* I do? Look for a job."

Stone frowned. "I don't mean to pry, John, but what skills do you have?"

"You know me well enough to know the answer to that one. None."

"What can I do to help you? I'll do anything."

John removed his hat and scratched his head. "Can't think of a thing. If I do, you'll be the first to know. But I appreciate your offer. Your friendship means a lot."

"Remember when we were riding out to meet the Kaws? You said you might lose your job over Stark's death?"

"Uh huh, I remember. What about it?"

"Remember what I said?" Stone grabbed the man's shoulder and stared straight into his eyes. "I said, 'Your family would be welcome to stay with me as long as necessary.'"

John grinned. "And I said, 'Even with three squalling infants?' Remember?"

The two men laughed together.

"Exactly. I meant it, John. Come and stay with me for as long as necessary. I'd welcome the company."

John's face grew somber. "As much as I appreciate the offer, Stone, I could never accept it. I'm an independent man, always have been. I would never take advantage of you." He climbed down from the wagon. "But, thanks. You're a good friend."

"Well, my door is open." Stone tugged on the reins and headed the horses back toward his ranch. "I think I'd better get these supplies to America, or I may have to come and live with you."

&

Juliette watched her father pace the floor from her place behind the counter. It'd been two weeks since the bank had rejected his request for a loan. She knew he'd checked out every job possibility in the area, and nothing seemed promising. Their situation was growing more critical each day. "I'm worried about Mother," she finally said. "I think she needs to see Doc Meeker."

"I know, but we can't take her. Not now."

"Can't? Why?"

He sank onto a chair, lowered his head into his hands, and rested his elbows on his knees. "We don't have money to pay Doc."

Juliette rushed to her father's side and put her arms about his shoulders. "Really?"

He lifted a weary gaze. "You're the only one I can talk to, Juliette. Since the bank turned down our loan, we can't buy the hotel. Our savings are nearly gone. Mrs. Stark has only given me to the end of the month. After that, we won't even have a roof over our heads."

Juliette gasped. She had no idea things were this bad. "What can I do to help? I'll do anything. Just name it." She felt her father's shoulders rise and fall, and she knew he was crying. She'd never seen him cry.

"I don't know. I just don't know. I'm all out of answers. I thought sure the Lord would provide a way. He's always taken care of us before. Where is He now?"

"Caroline and I are strong, Father. We've already told you we could get jobs. Maybe Thomas Ward would hire me to work in his store, and Reuben is able-bodied. He could—"

A frown blanketed John's face. "My daughter, work as a clerk in that store? Never. Too many ruffians go in there to buy supplies. Besides, with your mother's bad health, I need you here."

"But Father—"

"No, Juliette. That's my final word on the subject," he said so loudly she was afraid her mother would hear.

A knock sounded on the door. "Pretty late at night for folks to be out." John dabbed at his eyes, then nodded toward Juliette. "You go on to bed. I'll register whoever it is."

❧

"Evening, John. I know it's nearly eleven, but I've been thinking about you and your situation." Stone moved uneasily into the room. "I don't mean to pry, but I'm wondering if you've come up with a solution yet. You know—about buying the hotel."

John slowly seated himself, then leaned back and locked his hands behind his head with a deep sigh. "I not only can't get a loan, I can't even find a job."

Stone pulled a chair up next to him. "I've been thinking. I–I guess I could give you the money."

"*Give* me the money? You know I'd never let you do that. We're friends, but you've only known me a few months.

You'd be crazy to do such a foolish thing."

"Then I'll loan it to you. You can pay me interest."

John shook his head. "I have no collateral to offer you, nothing to secure the loan. No, Stone. I won't take charity, and that's exactly what it would be."

After an interminable silence, Stone spoke again. "Well then, I could buy the hotel, and you could run it for me."

John narrowed his eyes. "You, a rancher, buy the hotel? Don't be ridiculous. You're a better businessman than that. Besides, that wouldn't be any different than giving me the money outright or a loan without collateral!"

"All right, you won't let me give you the money, and you won't let me buy the hotel and let you run it." Stone twisted nervously in the chair, its wobbly legs creaking beneath his weight. "I—ah—may have another solution. One I've been thinking about ever since you got turned down at the bank. I hope you'll be interested."

Now he had John's full attention.

"Of course, I'm interested. I'm desperate. Tell me. What's your solution?"

"Your dilemma could provide an answer for both of us."

John straightened in his seat. "What, Stone? Tell me."

"I'll loan you the money to buy the hotel, interest free—if you get Juliette to marry me."

four

John jumped to his feet. "What did you say?"

"I said, get Juliette to marry me. It's a good solution for both of us, John. Hear me out."

John frowned. "I'm listening, but I don't like what I'm hearing. You want me to use my daughter as collateral?"

"Sit down," Stone demanded in a firm voice.

With a scowl, his friend sat down but kept his gaze pinned on Stone's face.

"I've—I've been thinking about your problem." Stone slowly lowered himself onto the sofa beside the distraught man. "I have a problem too. One I've never discussed with you."

John's scowl turned into a frown. "You have a problem? What has that got to do with asking Juliette to marry you? And how would that solve *my* problem?"

"Patience, John. Let me explain. As you know, I have two sons. They've been living with my sister in St. Joseph since—" He paused and swallowed hard. "Since Lucy—died. I'd like to bring them home. I've been putting it off because I felt incapable of being both mother and father to such young boys. I've even considered hiring a nanny—you know, someone to live in and care for my children and look after the house. But folks would talk, me being a widower."

"But you have America. Couldn't she—"

Stone laughed. "America? Do you realize how old America is? She's far too old to care for two rowdy boys. I need someone with a lot of spunk to look after my children, be a substitute mother, and handle things on the ranch like a wife would."

"Why don't you just marry one of the local women?" John asked with a shrug. "I can think of a dozen who would be happy to be your wife and live on your fine ranch."

Stone shot him an amused grin. " 'Cause I can't think of any of them I'd want to live with. That's important to me."

"But you said I should get Juliette to marry you. I don't understand. What does my daughter have to do with all of this?"

"She's the right age, she's bright, and she needs a home for her and her son. It'd be a marriage of convenience for both of us—a business arrangement. We could even draw up papers. It wouldn't be proper for me to hire a woman to come and live with me on the ranch, but no one would give it a second thought if I married her. I don't want a real wife."

"I don't—"

"Think about it. I could give your daughter the kind of life you want her to have. All she'd have to do in return is be a mother to my sons and take care of my home. That's it. And I'd give you the money to buy the hotel."

John stroked his face and stared off in space. "What about—"

"I wouldn't expect her to perform wifely duties, if that's what you're worried about. I'm not interested in her in that way. But I need help with my sons, and you need money. The end of the month is only a few days away."

"Even if I'd agree, she wouldn't do it, Stone. She's independent, that one. She has her mind set on marrying some fellow who'll whisk her off her feet like her first husband did. I know she won't settle for less. Besides, you're nearly twice her age. I doubt she thinks of you as marrying material."

"She would if she knew it would save the hotel for her family. That daughter of yours is loyal to you, John. She's told me time and time again how much she appreciated you allowing her to come along to Kansas. I think if you asked her, she just might do it. It'd be a good thing for that boy of hers too. She might do it for his sake."

John stared at the floor and rubbed at his chin. "I–I don't know. If she married you, it'd be for life."

"Look, John. I aim to take care of her and her son as long as I'm around this old earth. It's a good arrangement for all of us, and I'd be a good daddy to Andrew. You know how I love kids. If she ever wanted to leave me, I'd let her go."

John appeared thoughtful. "Would be good for her and her son, I have to admit."

"I want a fine Christian woman to raise my sons, and she's that kind of person."

John straightened. "You've talked to her about this?"

"Not exactly. I told her I was gonna ask for her hand in marriage someday. That's all."

John seemed surprised by his statement. "How did she respond? She never said a word about it to me."

Stone grinned. "I don't think she believed me."

John leaned back into the sofa and stretched out his legs. "I need time to think. This has come as quite a surprise."

"Take whatever time you need." Stone rose and headed for the door. "It's the best solution for everyone. All you have to do now is convince your daughter."

"I'm afraid Juliette won't take to this idea too kindly."

Stone pulled on his hat and stepped through the open doorway. "Then we'll have to convince her, won't we?"

ॐ

"You wanted to speak to me, Father?" Juliette asked as she came into the room.

After several anxious moments, John turned to his daughter. "You know the trouble I've been having. Financially."

She nodded with anticipation. "Yes, I know. Have you found someone to give you a loan?"

"Not exactly. But I have been offered a valid solution."

She clapped her hands. "Oh, Father. I knew you'd come through for us. What is your solution? Have you found a new job?"

John's heart pounded. "You're the solution, Juliette."

Huge inquisitive eyes lifted to his. "Me? How? You know I'll do anything I can to help. Just tell me."

"I—I know you'd like to find a fine man and marry again. Your son needs a father in his life, and—"

"Father? Tell me. What's your solution?"

"I–I don't think you'll want to know."

"Of course, I want to know. Andrew and I are a part of this family. Now, tell me."

"Juliette—" John closed his eyes, took a deep breath, and blurted it out. "I need you to marry Stone Piper."

Juliette stared at her father, her face reflecting her shock. "What did you say? Surely I didn't hear you right."

John blinked, then pressed his lips together in a straight line. "I–I said I need you to marry Stone Piper," he repeated.

"But why, Father? Why would you ask such a thing? Just a few minutes ago, we were talking about David and the importance of real love in our lives. I don't understand."

"I didn't want to ask you, but—" John pulled her to him and cradled her in his arms. "It's the only way, Daughter. Trust me. The only way."

"I'm confused." She lifted misty eyes to his. "The only way to what? Tell me. I don't know what you're talking about."

John breathed in a whiff of air to clear his head, then let it out slowly. He had to make her understand. "Remember when Stone came to me last night?"

She nodded.

"Since he's my friend, I'd confided in him about my financial difficulties. He'd offered to take our family into his home until I could get a job and we'd find a place of our own."

"But—what has that got to do with me—and marriage?"

"Patience, Daughter, I'm getting to that. It isn't easy for a man to talk to his daughter about his inability to provide for his family." He breathed in another gasp and continued. "I told Stone I appreciated his offer, but it would only be a temporary answer to a major problem. He came up with an idea that would help both of us."

"Marry me? How would that solve anything? And why would he want to marry me?"

He brushed the hair from Juliette's troubled face. "Yes, he wants to marry you. But," he hurried on to say, "it would be a marriage in name only. What he really needs is someone to be a mother to his boys and run his household. There would be no—"

"No love?"

"Right, no—ah, love. It would be a simple business agreement between the two of you. In exchange, Stone will provide for every need you and Andrew will ever have. Just think of it, Juliette: You'll live in a fine house, wear fine clothes, have all the things you've always wanted. You and your son would want for nothing. What a wonderful opportunity this would be for the two of you."

She pushed away and stared into his face. "But, Father, I don't understand. Why would you want me to do such a thing? You know I don't love him. What about all the talks you and I have had about love?"

He struggled with the words. "Be–because, if you marry Stone, he'll give me the money to buy the hotel, interest free."

Juliette backed off quickly. "You'd sell my life like this? Marry me to a man I don't love? To buy a hotel?"

He reached for her, but she screamed at him and shoved him away. "Never did I think my own father could be so cruel. I want no part of this plan of yours!" She gave him a cold stare. "Or did Stone come up with this idea?"

He touched her hand, but she pulled it away.

"Leave me alone. Don't even touch me! I won't do this! I won't! Do you hear me? I refuse to marry Stone Piper! I don't love him, and I will not marry him—no matter what!"

"It's okay, Daughter. Somehow I'll work things out. I had no right to ask this of you. It wasn't fair. Can you forgive your thoughtless old father?"

She curled up in the corner of the sofa and buried her face in her hands.

John sat down beside her, stroking her hair. "Please, Juliette? Please forgive me?" he begged softly. He'd never felt so low, so discouraged. Here he'd told his children he'd never allow them to help him support his family, and what was he doing? Asking his lovely daughter, his own flesh and blood, to give up her life to keep him from losing the hotel. "I'm so sorry. I wouldn't blame you if you hated me."

She lifted a tear-stained face. "I could never hate you, Father, and I do forgive you. I know how hard all of this has been on you, and I ask *your* forgiveness. I had no right to scream at you like that, under any conditions. But please, don't ask this of me. It's—it's too much."

She went on, "Think back to when David and I came to you, saying we wanted to get married. You lectured us about the importance of the marriage vows. How can you ask me to ignore those vows and marry someone as a business arrangement?"

"What's wrong? Juliette. Are you sick?" Caroline asked with a glance toward their father as she entered the lobby.

Juliette shook her head and placed her hand on her abdomen. "No—I—something just upset me."

John stared at Caroline for a moment. Then, after flashing a quick glance toward Juliette, he motioned for her to join them. "I have a problem, Caroline. Juliette and I have been discussing it. I hadn't planned to tell you—not yet, anyway. But you're eighteen now, and after thinking it over, I've decided you're old enough to handle it."

Without taking her gaze from her father, Caroline sat down by Juliette. "What is it, Father?"

"Mrs. Stark has put the hotel up for sale and—"

Caroline brightened. "We're buying it? The hotel is going to be ours?"

"No. I wish that were true. I've tried to buy it, but I can't raise the money. It appears we may be moving soon."

"But if you don't have the hotel, what will—?"

"I don't know what I'll do for employment, but I don't want you to worry about it. Don't say anything about this to the other children, and please don't discuss it with your mother. She has enough on her mind already. I just felt you should know." He rose and gave them each a smile.

"But, if you—"

He held up a hand. "That's all for now, Caroline. Now, go

check on your mother and see if she needs any help."

⋙

The clock chimed nine times as her father entered the hotel that night. Juliette was waiting at the door. "Where've you been? Mother has been sick with worry."

"Walking, mostly. I needed time to think. You haven't said anything to your mother or anyone about marrying Stone, have you?"

She shook her head. "No, I haven't. I was afraid you were going to tell Caroline this morning when you told her about the hotel."

"No, that part is between you and me and Stone. I've been chastising myself all day for entertaining such a foolish notion."

"It's not you I'm mad at, Father. It's Stone. How could he be so insensitive? To even offer such a thing to you was cruel, and to think he calls himself your friend."

He slipped the pad of his finger beneath her chin and lifted her face to his. "Don't say that, Juliette. Stone is a good friend. He only wanted to help. That's all. He never intended to cause any trouble. I'm sure of it."

"If he's such a good friend, he should just give you the money."

"He offered, but I refused. That's when he came up with this plan."

"The plan for you to sell me to him?" she asked indignantly.

Father flinched. "No, I'd never sell you to anyone. Please don't ever think that of me. That was never in my mind."

"Isn't that what you intended to do? Marry me off to him so he'd give you the money you need?" Her tone was once again accusatory.

"Oh, no, Child! You don't understand! Stone wants to bring his sons home to live with him. Unfortunately, in addition to running his ranch, his duties as deputy take him away from home for days at a time. America is too old to care for little boys. Stone needs someone younger to live in, care for them, and manage his household. Someone who can be with his children all the time."

"If he has that much money, why doesn't he just hire someone?"

"He could hire one of the local women, but he's too proper to have an unmarried woman living under his roof. Besides, a married woman would need to spend time with her family. He has his fine reputation to consider, so he came up with this idea. If you married him, he'd have someone to be a mother to his children and manage his house. You'd have everything you could ever want, and I'd have the money to buy the hotel and provide for my family. Really, Juliette, it's not as bad an idea as it seems. You and your son would have a wonderful life."

She listened but was not convinced.

"Please, don't be upset with Stone. If you're upset with anyone, let it be me. I'm the one who asked it of you—not him."

"Well—maybe you're right. But I won't blame you, Father. I know how hard this has been on you. I wish I could help, but you must understand, I cannot marry a man I don't love. I'd be miserable!"

John grabbed her hands and cupped them in his. "Please, let's forget I ever asked you to do such an unforgivable thing."

She stood on tiptoe and kissed her father's cheek. "But I will work at the general store, if it'll help."

"No, and that's final."

❧

The air was brisk in the quiet town of Dove City as Stone rode in on Blackie that night. Most folks had gone to bed, their lamps extinguished; but the lamp in the lobby of The Great Plains Inn burned brightly, and Stone knew his friend was toiling over the hotel's bookwork. He gave a slight tap on the windowpane and waited.

John opened the door and let him in. "I spoke with Juliette, and it didn't go well."

"She said no?" Stone pulled off his hat and sat down.

"She said a firm no. She was furious with both of us."

Stone leaned back and balanced his hat on his knee. "You explained it all to her?"

"Everything we'd discussed."

He rose and stuffed his hat onto his head. "Well, I guess that answers that. But don't forget my offer for your family to stay with me as long as necessary."

"I spoke with Robert Marquette at the bank this morning, and I'm sure you can guess what he said."

"Another no?"

"Another firm no. Almost as firm as Juliette's. I'd hoped he'd reconsider, but he said he couldn't take a chance on me without collateral."

Stone's brow creased. "What're you going to do?"

"I don't know. I just don't know. I've reached the end of my options."

Stone laid a hand on the man's shoulder. "I meant what I said. Your family is welcome at my house."

"Thanks, I may have to take you up on your offer."

"I'm still willing to give you the money."

John shook his head sadly. "You're a successful business-man, Stone. You didn't get that way by behaving foolishly. There'd be nothing in it for you. I couldn't let you do it."

"My offer still stands." Stone tipped his hat and rode away into the night with a heavy heart.

❧

Stone rose early the next morning. Each Sunday, he made a practice of arriving at the saloon ahead of the churchgoers to cover up the bars and arrange the chairs. Since Mr. Ward allowed the saloon to be used for public functions, church was one of them. It wasn't that Stone was a pillar of the church. He wasn't. But he'd attended services for so long, sometimes he felt like it. He rarely read his Bible and hardly ever prayed, though he bowed his head when others did. But he liked being around people who were good Christians. They were fine people with high moral standards, and he could trust them. He knew folks in the community took it for granted he was one of them, though he'd never outright claimed it.

He was just putting the last chair in place when the Baker family arrived. As the two men shook hands, Stone nodded a good morning to Mary Baker, then turned to Juliette. "Good morning."

She gave him a cold, emotionless stare and said nothing.

"You're looking beautiful this morning." He watched for a reaction to his compliment but didn't see one.

She moved past him and went to sit with her family in their regular place. He waited until the music began, then slipped into the empty chair beside her. When she made no effort to share her hymnal with him, he slid closer and took the corner of the book in his hand. Although she ignored him, he sang with his usual robustness, harmonizing occasionally with her lovely soprano voice. By the end of the service, he noticed she'd seemed to relax some, and he decided to chance speaking with her.

"Nice day for a drive in the country, don't you think?"

"Drive?" She eyed him suspiciously.

"I thought maybe you'd do me the honor of taking a ride with me this afternoon."

Furrows creased her brow. "I think not."

"Please, Juliette. I know your father talked to you about me. Give me a chance to explain my side of things."

"No need for explanations. My answer is no. Plain and simple, no. I want nothing to do with you." She tried to move away from him, but he slipped his hand under her elbow and firmly led her off to one side.

"I have to make you understand. I don't want there to be any hard feelings between us. Although we've only known each other for a few months now, your father is my friend." He glanced around, then continued, his voice even softer. "I want you to come and see my place. You've never been there."

She pulled away slightly, tugging from his grasp. "Why would I want to do that?"

"I've offered my home to your family if Mrs. Stark sells the hotel. I've tried to convince John there's plenty of room for everyone, but he's a proud man and very stubborn." He wanted to add, *Almost as stubborn as you!*

She relaxed a bit and seemed to be considering their housing dilemma.

"Come on, say yes. You can bring Andrew and Caroline. It's a beautiful day. I know you'd enjoy the ride."

She appeared to be giving it some thought. "That's the only reason you want me to come? Not to talk about marriage?"

"That's the only reason." Stone almost felt he should cross his fingers behind his back. That truly was the reason for his invitation, but he hoped when she saw his spread, she might decide to take him up on his offer, after all.

"Father told Caroline about the hotel, but he didn't tell either of us about your offer of housing. If she comes with me, I'll have to tell her, you know."

"I'm sure that'd be fine with your father, but perhaps you'd better get his approval first."

"I could ask him, but I don't want her to know about—"

"I know. I won't tell her."

"I guess it wouldn't hurt for us to see your place."

"You'll come?"

"If it's all right with Father."

"I'll come for you about three. You won't be sorry."

"I'd better not be." She shook a finger in his face. "This better not be a trick."

Stone crossed his fingers behind his back. "It's not."

❧

"You ladies comfortable back there?" Stone asked with a congenial smile, swiveling in his seat as the horses ambled up the dusty road. Juliette had refused his offer to ride up front with him, opting to sit in back with Caroline.

They'd barely reached the outskirts of town when Andrew began to fuss. Juliette knew her baby would not be satisfied until he was fed. Yet, how could she nurse him? Here in the buggy, with Mr. Piper sitting so close? She could feel a flush rise to her cheeks, just thinking about what she was about to do.

"Mr. Piper, I'm sorry, but my baby is hungry, and I must see to his needs. Would you—could you—please—face the front—for a little while?"

He sat up straight and squared his shoulders. "Ah, yes—certainly. Of course."

They rode along in silence as Andrew suckled beneath Juliette's shawl. When he finished, she handed him to Caroline. Once her clothing had been adjusted and put back into place, she leaned forward a bit. "Thank you, Mr. Piper."

He gave her a nod but kept his eyes on the road.

"Are you warm enough back there?" he asked finally. "I want you ladies to enjoy your ride."

"Thank you, Mr. Piper. We are. Are we getting near your place?" Caroline asked, craning her neck.

He turned in the seat to face his three passengers. "Actually, we've been on my place since before we crossed the bridge. The house is still up there a ways ahead of us."

Caroline scanned the area. "This land is all yours?"

"Sure is. A mighty lot to keep up."

"But you do have help, right?" she asked, obviously impressed with the magnitude of what she was seeing.

Stone let out a hearty laugh. "Lots of help. I could never take care of all of this by myself."

"Could you hire our father to work for you?"

"Wish I could, Miss Caroline, but my work is seasonal. Your pa needs something he can work at every day."

"Oh, I see." She seemed disappointed.

"See over there through the trees? The Neosho River runs across my land. Makes a good swimming hole in the summer and provides water for my stock.

"Look, you can barely see the roof of my house. And over that way are the barns. Down there is the cabin where America and Moses live."

"Your slaves?" Caroline asked with big eyes as she glanced

in the direction of the old couple's cabin.

"Slaves? No!" Stone stated emphatically. "They're friends who happen to work for me."

"I heard Mrs. Marquette say they're your slaves."

"No, Caroline. Those two are as free as you or I."

"Then why would Mrs. Marquette say such a thing?" Juliette asked.

"The story probably got all messed up. My father did buy Moses and America, and they *were* his slaves. But my father died a long time ago. The first thing I did after I claimed his property was to set them free."

"If they're free, why are they still with you?"

"It's their choice, Caroline. They wanted to come to Kansas, and since I'd never known life without them, I wanted them here with me. I made it perfectly clear to them that they were no longer slaves of the Piper family. They were my employees, and as employees, they were free to come and go at any time."

Caroline smiled. "Oh, that's so wonderful. What a nice man you are, Mr. Piper."

"Tell that to your sister. I don't think she agrees."

Juliette lowered her gaze and avoided his eyes. "I do think you're a nice man, Stone. It's just that I—"

He reached back and cupped his hand over hers. "I know. You don't have to explain."

The buggy slowly rounded a curve in the road, and Stone's house could be seen in the distance. "We're nearly there," he explained as he gave the reins a gentle flip.

"Oh, my, I've never seen such a huge house," Caroline exclaimed as they moved up the lane. "Do you live here alone?"

Stone nodded. "All alone, but I have two sons living in St. Joseph. I plan to bring them home as soon—" He cast a quick glance at Juliette. "As soon as it's possible."

"Oh, Juliette. This is the kind of house we were wishing for, remember?"

Juliette gave her sister a frown. "I don't know what you're talking about."

"Yes, you do. We said maybe we could both marry rich men and ride around in fancy buggies while other women did our work for us. Surely you remember. We were standing in the hotel lobby. You were saying—"

"I said I don't remember, Caroline. Please, let's not discuss this now."

Stone grinned to himself. *So, Juliette was talking about marrying a rich man. Could that have been after I gave her Lucy's handkerchief and told her I planned to marry her?*

Caroline let out a sigh. "If you say so."

Time to change the subject. He didn't want Juliette to be upset about anything. He wanted her mind to be on the advantages he could give her if she married him. He made a large circle around the outbuildings, passed by America and Moses' cabin, then turned into the circle drive in front of the spacious house. "Here we are."

He leaped from the buggy and rushed around to assist his guests. After handing Andrew to Caroline, his fingers circled Juliette's waist, and he slowly lifted her down. His eyes never left her lovely face. "There you go, little lady."

She gave him a demure smile that made him grin, and he tipped his hat. *Maybe she isn't as mad at me as I thought.*

"Juliette, look at this place. It's the biggest house I've ever seen! Bigger'n any in Ohio." Caroline spun around, looking in all directions. "Wouldn't you like to live here?"

"Yes," Stone asked with a wink as he took Andrew from Caroline and ushered Juliette up the steps of the wraparound porch. "Wouldn't you like to live here, Juliette?"

With a quick snap of her head, she turned to face him, hostility in her eyes. "For a few weeks maybe. No longer."

"I could live here forever!" Caroline said as she hurried up the steps ahead of them.

America met them at the door, wearing a freshly laundered apron.

"Juliette. Caroline. This is America."

America gave them each a nod, then slipped a brown finger

into the sleeping baby's chubby hand. "Would you like to lay him down?"

Juliette leaned toward her and whispered, "I nursed him on the way. It's time for his nap, so he'll probably stay asleep for an hour or so."

America pointed to a small daybed in the far corner. "He should be comfortable there. Push that chair up close so he won't roll off."

The three watched as Juliette carefully placed her son on the daybed and tucked the blanket about his shoulders. "Thank you, America," Juliette said as she moved back across the room.

Caroline stared openmouthed at the oversized room, then turned to America. "Mr. Piper said you used to be a slave."

Juliette's hand reached out to cover her sister's mouth.

"It's okay," Stone advised with a laugh. "I don't think America minds talking about it, do you, America?"

"No, I don't mind." She turned to their inquisitive guest. "I used to be Stone's pa's slave, but never Stone's. He freed me and Moses the day he got everything."

Caroline turned to her sister. "Isn't that nice, Juliette? Isn't Stone the nicest man you ever met?"

"Yes, very nice," Juliette agreed sullenly.

"Stone asked me to cook up his favorite little cakes and some tea. Would ya like some?" the old woman asked.

"Of course, they would," Stone answered for them, "as soon as I've shown them the rest of the house."

"Why did you ever build such a big house, Mr. Piper?" Caroline asked as they moved through a hallway and into the master bedroom.

"For my wife," he explained proudly. "Lucy wanted a showy house with fine furniture. I built it just like she wanted it."

"Caroline, don't ask so many questions," Juliette cautioned with a warning frown. "You're being rude."

"It's all right. I don't mind answering. That's why I invited you here today. I wanted us to get to know each other better." Turning to Caroline, he went on. "She died. My Lucy died not long after my second son's birth."

"Oh, that's terrible!" Caroline returned with a frown as she put a consoling hand on the man's arm. "I'm so sorry."

"So am I," Stone agreed. "I loved her very much. Life hasn't meant much to me since she's been gone."

"Why don't your boys live with you?" Caroline asked.

Again her sister gave her a warning frown.

"I want them to, but boys their age need a woman to take care of them. Since I haven't found that woman—" He shot another glance toward Juliette. "Since I haven't found that woman, they've stayed in St. Joseph with my sister."

Caroline nodded toward America. "Couldn't she take care of them?"

"Stone won't let me," America answered as she scurried toward the kitchen.

"She's an *old* woman," Stone added with a hearty laugh. "Too old for two rowdy boys. I couldn't ask that of her."

"You could hire someone who wasn't that old," Caroline continued.

"Wouldn't look right for a woman to be living out here on the ranch with a widower." Stone turned toward Juliette, and this time she was looking directly at him.

"Couldn't you find a wife?" Caroline asked with a glance toward her sister, as if she expected Juliette to silence her once more.

He reared back with a vigorous laugh. "I thought I'd found one, but she said no."

"She must be crazy!" Caroline sat down in a well-padded chair, testing the cushion's plumpness. "Can you imagine it, Juliette? Some woman would say no to all of this?"

"Yes, crazy," Juliette answered softly with a piercing glare toward her host.

"Juliette, would you look at this bedroom?" Caroline followed close at Stone's heels. "This is your bedroom, Mr. Piper?"

Stone nodded. "Like it? Lucy fixed it this way."

Caroline leaned over the bed and ran her fingers across the

delicate quilt. "I wish I had a bed like this."

They moved on to the room across the hall, a smaller room but quite nice, filled with ladylike furniture. Everything with lace. Even the pillowcases had lace edges. A beautiful quilt with appliquéd flowers covered the bed. "Lucy made that quilt," Stone explained. "She liked to do handwork."

"It's lovely," Juliette admitted with admiration as her fingers traced the swirling green vines that connected the flowers. "You must have loved her very much."

"I did," he conceded. "No one will ever take her place."

"Not even the lady who said *no* when you asked her to marry you?" Caroline asked as she bent to look at a delicate glass vase on the table beside the bed.

"Not even her," he told her with another wink to her sister. "Let me show you the other bedroom on this floor. It's the room I'm going to fix up for—" He paused. "Whoever takes care of my boys."

As they made their way down the hall, Caroline clasped her hand on the knob of a closed door near Stone's bedroom. "Whose room is this?"

Stone quickly moved to the door and placed his back against it. "Storeroom. I–I have things in there that—"

"It's none of our business," Juliette stated sharply as she tugged at her sister's sleeve.

"It's all right," Stone said, interceding. "It's nothing important, Caroline. Really. Just a storeroom. I'm sure you wouldn't want to see it. Let me show you the other bedroom." He ushered them into the smallest of the rooms. "Not much to see in here. Mostly, I just use it as a place to keep my books, though I don't have much time to read." He moved back into the hall. "Let's go upstairs."

Caroline's eyes widened. "You have a bedroom upstairs too?"

Stone's booming laugh filled the house. "Caroline, I have three bedrooms upstairs. That's why I told your father I have plenty of room for your family to come and stay with me."

Caroline climbed the stairs, keeping a full step ahead of their long-legged host.

"Only if Father doesn't buy the hotel or get a job," Juliette explained quickly.

They toured the upstairs bedrooms, then made their way into the kitchen to enjoy the cakes and tea America had prepared. "Look who woke up!" America said, holding Andrew in her arms.

"Hi, Precious." Juliette reached out to take him. "Did you have a good nap?"

"He sure looks like it." Stone pointed toward Andrew's smiling face. "You're a happy baby."

America placed the platter on the table. "I hope you like these."

"America is the best cook in the world," Stone commented as he moved to her side and planted a kiss on the little round bun of hair secured to the top of her head.

She grinned. "That man is just used to my cookin'. He don't know no better."

Caroline moved quickly to the table, pulled out a chair, and seated herself. But Juliette waited until Stone pulled her chair out for her in true gentlemanly fashion.

Once they were gathered around the table, America filled their cups with freshly brewed tea.

"This is good," Caroline commented as she bit into one of the tasty cakes. "Do you fix these for Stone often?"

"I've fixed these cakes for Stone since he was two years old," America said with a kindly look toward her employer. "They're his favorites."

Everyone laughed when Andrew's chubby hand reached for a cake as America handed the platter to Juliette.

After they'd finished their tea and cakes, Stone motioned for them to follow him. "I nearly forgot to show you the special room I built on for Lucy. It was her favorite."

He led them through a small door off the kitchen. In the middle of the cozy room sat a large wooden tub. On a table nestled next to it, a row of candles lay in a delicate china dish, along with a tiny bar of French soap molded into the shape of a flower.

"This was your wife's bath?" Juliette asked incredulously as her eyes scanned the intimate little room set into an alcove. "Her very own bath?"

"Only hers."

Juliette stared at the small stack of towels lying beside the rosebud-trimmed china washbowl and pitcher. "This is so nice."

"This smells wonderful," Caroline commented as she picked up the sweetly scented bar of soap and touched it to her cheek. "Wouldn't you like to have a room like this, Juliette?"

Juliette flashed an uncomfortable glance toward Stone, then quickly turned away as their eyes met. "Of course. What woman wouldn't?"

Stone took a quick step up behind her and whispered in her ear. "It could be yours, Juliette. All of this could be yours, if you'd just say yes."

five

Juliette moved away quickly. Obviously, no matter how appealing his house seemed or how much money he may have in the bank, she could not, and would not, even entertain the thought of marrying him.

He wished he'd kept his suggestion to himself. He hadn't meant to offend her. He'd simply wanted her to see the advantages for everyone concerned if she'd marry him.

Juliette gazed out the window, turning her back on him.

Stone wanted to follow her to apologize, but Caroline kept going on about Lucy's bath and asking him all sorts of questions.

Finally, he pulled a folded paper from his pocket and moved back to the kitchen table. "Now this is the way I figured we could house the Baker family."

At first, Juliette continued to stare off in space as if she had no interest in his plan. But as he pointed to each square on the chart and talked about where each family member would be housed, she couldn't help but listen. She asked Caroline to change Andrew's diaper, then joined Stone at the table.

"And I thought this small room on the first floor at the end of the hall would be good for you and Andrew, Juliette. There's a nice feather bed in there. That way, you won't have any stairs to climb with that heavy boy in your arms. Is that suitable for you?"

"Ah—yes, ah—anything would be fine if Father doesn't find a job by the end of the month. But I'm sure he will."

Stone checked to make sure Caroline couldn't hear as his face grew solemn. "The end of the month is nearly here. Even if he were to find a job tomorrow, he would most likely not get paid for two weeks. From what John has told me, his money is nearly gone," he said in a near whisper.

"I know. He told me too," she confessed meekly.

"Plans need to be made now."

"I told him, if we have to move, I could go work in Mr. Ward's store," Juliette inserted. "I might not make much money, but whatever I made, he could have."

Stone reared back with a frown. "Do you honestly think your father would allow you to work in that store? A fine young lady like you has no business dealing with the men who go in there for supplies."

"Women go in there too, and if I want to work at that store, Father would have to allow it," she answered with an indignant tilt of her chin. "I *am* an adult."

"Well, that's between you and John. If we were honest, I think we both know what his decision would be."

"I'm ready to go home now," Juliette announced as Caroline came back into the room. She grabbed up her cape, snatched Andrew from her sister's arms, and headed out the door. "You have a fine house, Mr. Piper. But hopefully, Father will work something out and refuse your offer."

Stone turned to Caroline. "Stay here with America. Give me a few minutes to speak with your sister."

Caroline nodded.

He found Juliette standing on the porch, attempting to wrap her cape about her shoulders and hold Andrew at the same time. He stepped forward and took the baby from her arms as he motioned toward a bent willow bench. "Please, Juliette. I didn't mean to offend you. Sit down and let's talk. I want you to understand my position in all of this."

She crossed her arms and turned away from him.

"Please?"

Slowly, she moved to the bench and seated herself. Stone sat down beside her with the baby contentedly snuggled up in the crook of his arm. "Look. Your father and I haven't known each other for very long, but he's my friend. I'd do anything to help him through this hard time. I even offered to give him the money to buy the hotel outright. But he refused to take it."

Her gaze lifted to meet his. "You offered to give him the money? Really?"

"Yes. As his friend, I wanted to help. But he wouldn't take it."

"That's when you came up with this ridiculous marriage idea?"

He thoughtfully smoothed at the baby's hair before answering. "Actually, I came up with the marriage idea several months ago. I've wanted to bring my boys home for such a long time. I think you can understand that. Being separated from them all these years has been hard on them and on me."

She smiled at her baby, and he smiled back. "Then why didn't you?"

"Who would take care of them? I'm outside working my ranch from before the sun comes up most days, and what days I'm not, I'm repairing barns and tools, helping other ranchers, or performing my duties as deputy. Those boys need someone to be with them all the time. America's too old to care for two growing, energetic boys. I couldn't ask that of her."

"You could hire someone."

"I've thought of that many times. But who would I hire? One of the local women with a family of her own to tend to? Someone who would go home at the end of the day?"

She grew thoughtful. "Carrie Sullivan could probably do it. She's not much over twenty and would be good to your boys."

"Carrie Sullivan is a single woman. Do you think it would look proper for someone like that to live in my house?"

Her gaze lowered. "No, I guess not."

"Now you're beginning to see my problem. I don't want a nanny and a housekeeper for my sons. They deserve more than that."

She looked up into his eyes. "Then what do you want, Stone?"

He grinned. "You. You're the perfect solution."

"Me?" She jumped to her feet and snatched the nearly sleeping baby from his arms, her face flushed and angry. "I'm the answer for you, maybe, and perhaps for Father. But I won't be anyone's solution, Mr. Piper. I'm not a slave you can buy and sell at your whim."

He rose awkwardly, knowing he'd used the wrong words. Again. "I did not buy America or Moses. You know that. I would never attempt to buy another human being."

She rushed down the steps toward the buggy, nearly tripping on the last step, with Stone at her heels. "Never? You just did, Mr. Piper. You tried to buy me!"

"No, that was not my intention! Why can't you understand my motives?" Frustrated, he stood on the bottom step, his arms dangling limply at his sides. It'd been years since he'd argued with a woman, and he found himself speechless and inadequate.

"Oh, I understand your motives all right," she quipped angrily as she struggled to put the baby into the buggy's seat and climb up herself without assistance. "Your motives are very clear. You need a mother for your boys, and you're willing to buy one. Well, let me tell you, Stone Piper: You will not buy this woman. Juliette Baker Martin is not for sale."

"But—"

Andrew began to cry at the top of his lungs, nearly drowning out their conversation. "But—nothing, Mr. Piper. Now, if you'd be so kind, I'd like to go home. All this bargaining is giving me a headache." With that she squared her shoulders, lifted her chin, and stared straight ahead, ignoring his pleas.

"Caroline," Stone called out loudly. "You can come out now. Your sister is ready to go home."

Silence permeated the air all the way back into town. No one seemed to have anything to say.

Occasionally, Stone would sneak a peek at the girls. Each time, he'd wish he'd been more diplomatic in his approach of the marriage subject. *You're a fool*, he told himself as the buggy rolled toward town, *to even think that lovely young woman would consider spending the best and most productive years of her life with you, taking care of your children, when she could have her pick of men.*

He circled the buggy around and came to a stop near the hotel's door. He hurried to assist Juliette, but she refused his hand and lowered herself to the ground before reaching for her baby. He followed the three of them into the hotel where John was waiting.

John greeted them warmly. "What did you think of Stone's place, girls?"

Still wide-eyed, Caroline was the first to answer. "Oh, Father, it is so pretty. I've never seen such a fine house."

He turned to Juliette. "What did you think?"

Stone pulled his hat from his head and rotated its brim nervously between his fingers with a sheepish grin toward her. "There's plenty of room for the Baker family, right?"

She moved toward the stairs. "Yes, I guess so, but not for me. I'm sure Andrew and I can find a place with one of the members of our church."

"Want me to change Andrew's diaper?" Caroline asked, reaching out toward the smiling baby. "I'm going upstairs."

Juliette gave her an appreciative grin. "Would you mind?"

Caroline took Andrew and cuddled him in her arms. "Not a bit."

As soon as she'd reached the top of the stairs, John stepped out and took hold of Juliette's arm. "You and Andrew aren't going anywhere. We're a family. Where one goes, we all go. That includes the two of you."

Ignoring their guest, she turned to face him, her eyes burning their way into his. "But you'd let me go and marry a man I don't love? Move away from my family so you can keep your precious hotel? I think not, Father." She pulled away and followed her sister up the stairs. "You'll have to excuse me. I have to feed my son."

Stone bowed his head in defeat. "Sorry, John. Guess I didn't handle things too well."

"Not your fault. You tried. She's right though. I guess I *am* willing to sell her to keep the hotel."

"No, that's not true. None of us wants to put Juliette's happiness on the line. You want the best for her, and so do I. I could give her the kind of life she's always wanted." He let his shoulders slump. "Oh, I know I'm not the kind of man she wants for a husband, but I'd be good to her, John. I'd give her anything she wants. . .except love. I can't give her that. My heart still belongs to Lucy. But your daughter would never want for anything."

John put his hand on Stone's shoulder. "I know that. You're a good man."

"That daughter of yours is as stubborn as they come. Did you know she's planning on getting a job at Mr. Ward's store?"

"So she says, but I say no. I forbid it."

"She's an adult. What could you do to stop her? Women are doing strange things nowadays."

"I know, and that's what worries me. But if I can't provide for her and Andrew, what say do I have?"

"None, it appears. But she respects you, John. She'd never do anything to embarrass you or her family."

"I'm counting on that. I finally told Reuben about our financial condition. I hate to keep things from the family. By the way, thanks for bringing the girls home."

"You do know I'll give you the money, even if Juliette refuses to marry me, don't you?"

John nodded. "Yes, I know. But I can't take it—not without you getting something in return."

⁂

Juliette stood at the top of the stairs, listening. How could her father and Stone expect her to marry a man she didn't love? David had been the love of her life, but their time together had been so short. Surely somewhere she could find another man who would love her as David had—a man who could sweep her off her feet and make her spine tingle at his touch. One she could give herself to wholeheartedly.

She listened as her father and her suitor discussed the money her father needed. She marveled at Stone's generosity when he offered to give them his hard-earned money. Not many men would do such an unselfish thing. He'd be a good catch for any woman. If only she loved him.

જય

Stone jammed his hat on his head, then untied the horses from the hitching post and climbed into the wagon. "Women!" he said aloud as he whipped the reins and headed toward the ranch.

જય

"Juliette, Caroline. Wake up!" Her father's voice pierced the darkened room. "Your mother needs you!"

Juliette sat up and rubbed at her eyes. "What time is it?"

"Nearly four. Hurry!"

She grabbed her robe and wrapped it around her, pulled the coverlet over her sleeping baby, and hurried down the narrow hall to her parents' room. Her father was bending over the bed, hovering over her mother. "What's wrong with her?"

"She started feeling poorly right after you girls left with Stone yesterday afternoon. I didn't tell you last night."

"Did you call Doc Meeker?"

He shook his head and whispered his response. "No, I wanted to, but she didn't want me to call him. I think she knew we didn't have the money to pay him. I shouldn't have listened to her."

"Go get him," Juliette ordered as she bent over the bed and stroked her mother's fevered brow.

John nodded and disappeared.

The two girls kept vigil and prayed over their mother until John returned with Doc Meeker.

"How long has she been like this?"

"She had a bad spell yesterday afternoon. She started vomiting, and she's been having terrible headaches," John explained as he rubbed the pad of his thumb over his wife's frail hand. "She hasn't felt well since the twins were born."

"Why didn't you send someone for me?"

"I—ah. She— We—we didn't have the money to pay you."

The doctor stopped his examination and stared at John. "This is your wife's health we're talking about. I'm a doctor, not a banker. She seems very weak. I hate to tell you this, but the best thing you could do for her is send her somewhere where she can have constant bed rest for a few weeks. I think the woman's problem is exhaustion."

John rubbed at his temples and nodded. "It's my fault. If I'd had any idea she was carrying twins, I would never have left Ohio. Her other births had been such easy ones; neither of us expected this last time to be any different."

"Picking up and moving such a long way, tending to the needs of her family, then having the babies—" Doc paused. "I think all of it has taken a toll on her, John. Look how thin she's become. She's nothing but skin and bones."

"She isn't going to die, is she?" Juliette blurted out.

The doctor spun around to face her. "No, Juliette. But if she doesn't get away from the responsibilities and pressures of her life here at the hotel, I doubt she's going to get any better. This woman needs rest. Uninterrupted rest."

"But how—"

Doc Meeker lifted a hand. "I know what your family has been going through, but it's Mary's life we're talking about here, and—"

"Mary's aunts live about fifty miles away. They've been wanting her to come for a visit." John wiped at his eyes with his sleeve. "Do you think she could stand the trip?"

"Yes, if you make sure she can lie down most of the way," Doc advised. "The sooner you can take her there, the better."

"Since Mary is nursing the twins, we'll have to take them with us, but I'm sure her aunts will be able to handle them."

"Maybe you could send one of the girls along to help out," Doc suggested.

John smiled. "Good idea. I'll send Molly along. She's only eight, but she's a good helper and the twins love her."

"Just so long as Mary gets the rest she needs. That's the important thing," Doc added.

John nodded. "Fine. I'm sure Caroline and Juliette can help us pack. We'll leave as soon as we can get ready. "

"What's to become of us?" Caroline asked her sister as the buggy disappeared. "First the hotel. Now this."

"Good question," Reuben stated as he echoed his sister's fears. "Father's already been at his wit's end."

Juliette let out a deep sigh and squished her eyes shut tightly. "The Baker family needs a miracle."

☙

By ten o'clock Juliette had risen, fed Andrew, dressed him, turned his care over to Caroline, and was walking down Main Street toward the Stark home. She'd never begged before, but if begging would help, she'd do it.

Mrs. Stark answered the door almost immediately.

Juliette moved past her into the well-furnished parlor. "I've come to ask for more time to buy the hotel."

The woman began to shake her head. "I'm sorry, Dear. I simply can't do it. There is someone ready to buy it in case your father doesn't come up with the money. I need to get this settled."

"No, you can't sell it to someone else. He needs that hotel!"

"I'm sorry, Dear, but this buyer is willing to give me more money than your father had offered. I'm afraid I have no choice but to sell it to him."

"But, Mrs. Stark, my mother is sick. My father just left to take her fifty miles away to the home of two of her aunts, where she can rest and get the care she needs. You know how poorly she's felt since we arrived in Dove City. He can't possibly be back in time to come up with the money by your deadline!"

"I'm sorry to hear about your mother, but I must think of myself and my own family."

Juliette jumped to her feet. "You've given him to the end of the month. He had your word on it. His time isn't up yet."

"The end of the month is only a few days away. I'm sorry. That's all the time I can give him."

Furious at the woman, she turned and rushed out into the morning air.

ᴥ

With a small bundle tucked under one arm and an apology in his heart, Stone mounted Blackie and headed for town.

As he passed the Stark house on Main Street, the door burst open and Juliette came bustling out. He called to her, but she didn't seem to hear. Leaping off Blackie, he quickly tied him to a hitching post and hurried after her.

He caught up to her nearly a half a block farther, and to his surprise, she literally flung herself into his arms. He pulled her close, unsure of the reason for his good fortune.

"Oh, Stone, Mother had a bad spell when we were at your house. You know how thin she is. She hasn't been well since the twins were born. Doc Meeker said he thinks she needs rest to get well. She needs to get away from the busy demands of her everyday life. Away from us." She buried her head in his chest, deep sobs wracking her body. "I think the worry about Father's job has been too much for her. She's exhausted. She hasn't been eating or sleeping, she's—"

"What's your father going to do? Where would she go?"

"Some of Mother's relatives live about fifty miles away. They've been wanting Mother to come for a visit. They're both widows and don't have children at home, so it will be peaceful and quiet there. Father fixed up a bed in his buggy. They left early this morning."

"Oh, Juliette, I'm so sorry. If only I'd known. How's your father taking it? What did Doc say?"

"Father took it pretty hard, but he was brave for Mother. We're all worried. She looked so pale—"

He wrapped his arms tightly about her, wishing he could do something to make things better. "I want to help. What can I do?"

She lifted misty eyes to his. "Marry me!"

six

Stone grasped Juliette's shoulders and stared at her delicate, tear-stained face in disbelief. "Mar–marry you? I—is that what you said?" *Is God answering my prayer already?*

Her body trembled, and she pursed her lips before answering. "Yes—that's exactly what I said."

He held her at arm's length. "Why were you at Mrs. Stark's house?"

She hung her head. "Begging for more time."

"And she refused, I take it?"

"Worse than that. She said she had another buyer ready to sign the contract for more money than Father was going to give her."

"So that's why you've had a change of heart. You've decided to marry me so your father can buy the hotel."

She bit her lower lip and avoided his eyes. "Yes, if you'll still have me."

Stone grew sullen. "I told your father I'd give him the money. Talk him into taking it, and you won't have to marry me."

"He won't take it. Please, Stone. Father won't be home for several days. By then, it'll be past the end of the month and too late. But you could close the sale yourself and take the money to Mrs. Stark." She lifted her gaze until it met his. "I promise I'll marry you, and I'll be a good wife."

"I–I don't know," he said hesitantly as he eyed her. "I think we're all asking too much of you. Especially me."

She lifted her hand and stroked his cheek. "No, Stone. Not you. I see that now. Your motives are pure. You've asked so little in return. It is I who's been selfish. You've not only offered me a fine home for my son and myself and all that goes with it, but you're making it possible for my family to keep the hotel. I'm asking for *your* forgiveness."

He leaned away in surprise. "My forgiveness? There's nothing to forgive. I was coming to apologize to you and ask for *your* forgiveness!"

"I'll be a good mother to your boys, and I'll run your house the best I can. I know I'll never be as good at it as your Lucy, but I'll try. Please, Stone. Marry me!"

"You'll do just fine," he assured her as he lifted her hand to his lips and kissed it. "I want you to know I'll never expect—" He fumbled around for the words.

She laughed through her tears. "I know—and I trust you."

He stood proudly, his head held high. "I'll go to the bank now and have Marquette draw up the papers. I'll sign them on John's behalf and have the money transferred to Mrs. Stark's account. By the time your father gets back home, your family will own the hotel."

Juliette's hands covered her face as she wept. "I'm so grateful, Stone. Father said you were a good man, and you are." Slowly, she looked up into his eyes. "When shall we be married?"

He gave her a victorious grin. "As soon as your mother is able to come to the wedding."

She smiled, asking through her tears, "Do you want a small wedding? With just our families?"

"Nope. Want a big one. Let's invite everyone in the community. I want to do it up right."

"Of course, your sister and your sons will come in time for the wedding, won't they?"

The corners of his mouth turned up, causing crinkly lines to form by his eyes. "Yep, I can hardly wait for them to meet my bride."

"I'm excited about meeting them too. I'm sure they're fine boys. They're yours."

He reared back with a laugh. "Can't take credit for their upbringing, but I'm sure my sister is doing a fine job. You know I'll be a good father to Andrew, don't you? I love that boy already."

Her hand quickly covered her mouth. "Andrew! I almost forgot. I left Caroline taking care of the children, and Reuben is working at the front desk by himself. He needs to do his chores. I have to get home."

He reached for her hand. "I'll walk you there."

"But—" She gestured toward Blackie, still tied up to the post.

"He's got nothing better to do. He'll wait."

a

After Stone had seen Juliette safely back to the hotel, he walked to where he had hitched Blackie to the post. After making sure the gelding was still secured properly, he walked down the street to the bank.

Robert Marquette greeted him with a handshake as he entered. "What can I do for you today?"

"I need you to draw up a contract for me, Robert," he answered, towering over the man.

The bank president motioned toward his big oak desk. "Gonna buy some more land, are you, Stone?"

"You might say that."

Mr. Marquette pulled some papers from a drawer, then dipped his pen in the inkwell. "I hope you have the legal description."

"Nope, but I'm sure you do. I want the papers drawn up in John Baker's name. He's buying The Great Plains Inn."

Mr. Marquette quit smiling. "I turned down his request for a loan, Stone. He has no collateral."

"He doesn't need collateral, Robert. He has the money. Right here in your bank."

The man shook his head sadly. "No, I'm afraid you're wrong. I'm afraid John Baker would be hard-pressed to come up with enough to buy a new sofa for the inn, let alone purchase the building."

Stone pointed to the paper. "The contract, Robert. Write it up, or would you rather I take John's business elsewhere?"

The man hesitated. "This seems like a waste of time, since I haven't seen John's money."

"You want to see the money?" Stone stood to his feet and pounded a fist on the man's desk, his patience wearing thin. "Then go into your vault and pull it out of my account. I'm covering it for John!"

The banker leaned back in his chair and stared at him. "You're covering it? All of it? Do you realize how much money we're talking about here? John has absolutely no collateral."

Stone stared the man down. "Do you realize it's my money and I can spend it any way I choose?"

"You're sure about this?" the man prodded with concern.

Stone sat back down. "If I wasn't sure, would I be here asking you for a contract?" He pointed to the pen. "Write."

❧

Juliette sat in front of the window, staring into space. *Well, I've done it. I've committed my life to Stone Piper.* She lowered her head and closed her eyes. *Oh, God, am I doing the right thing? I need Your assurance. Please, give me some sort of sign. This is not at all what I expected from life. I want to do Your will. Guide me, please. Draw me close to You.*

"Juliette! Are you up there?" Caroline called to her from the lobby. "Someone is here to see you."

She wiped at her eyes and smoothed her hair, then checked her sleeping baby before heading down the stairs.

"Got something for you," Stone said with a big smile that all but covered his ruddy face. "Here."

Juliette moved toward him. "For me? What?"

He continued to grin. "Actually, I have two things for you. This morning when I rode into town, I was bringing you this." He handed her the china dish containing several bars of the delicate French soap from Lucy's bath. "As a peace offering. But when I heard about your mother, I forgot to give it to you."

Juliette took one of the sweetly scented bars and held it to her nose, breathing in the wonderful fragrance. "What a lovely gift. How thoughtful of you. Thank you." She felt herself blushing.

"I have another gift for you," Stone said, beaming at her,

a broad smile covering his face. "You're going to like this one too."

"Oh, Stone. Two gifts in one day. You're spoiling me."

He gave her a sly wink. "I intend to keep spoiling you. You *and* Andrew." He pulled a folded paper from his jacket pocket and handed it to her. "Here's your other surprise."

She carefully unfolded the legal-looking paper and began to read while Stone looked on. When she reached the end, tears exploded from her eyes. "Oh!"

"What is it, Juliette? Why are you crying?" Caroline asked as she hurried into the room. "What have you done to upset my sister?"

"I'm not upset, I'm happy!" Juliette grabbed Caroline's arms and swung her about the room. "Stone purchased this hotel for our father! Mrs. Stark has already signed the bill of sale!"

"You did. You've bought the hotel? Oh, Mr. Piper, I love you. You're an angel!" Caroline said happily.

Juliette laughed with amusement. "Careful there, little sister. You're making Mr. Piper blush."

"I've been called a lot of things, but never an angel."

"Well, you're our angel." Caroline grinned as she climbed the stairs. "Wait'll Father and Mother get home and hear about this!"

"You can keep thinking that, if you want to!" he called out with a chuckle before turning to Juliette. "I'd best be going. If you need anything before your father gets back, just send Reuben, and I'll come running. I mean that, Juliette." He bent and whispered in her ear, "You're my family now."

"You're my family too."

"You and I'll get together soon to discuss our plans. That is, if you're still willing to go through with our marriage."

"Of course, I am! Can you have supper with us tomorrow night?" she offered. "I'm fixing bean soup, and I'm pretty good at it."

"Bean soup, eh? That's one of my favorites. With cornbread?"

"With cornbread."

"I'll be here." He stepped away, nearly stumbling over a chair. "About six?"

"Six is fine." Juliette watched him go. In a matter of hours, Stone had managed to turn the Baker family's life around. Hers, as well. He was quite a man. She was sure he'd make a fine husband.

If only she loved him.

⁂

Reuben stepped out from behind the counter in the hotel lobby and extended his hand. "Juliette said you were coming for supper. We're having bean soup. It's one of the few dishes my sister can cook."

Stone smiled as he removed his hat and hung it on a peg. "With cornbread, right?"

Reuben shrugged. "Yeah, I guess so. She's been scurrying around all afternoon, setting and resetting the table. You'd think a general was comin' to eat with us." He led the way through the hall and into the kitchen with Stone at his heels.

"Oh! You're early." Juliette quickly untied the apron from about her waist and began fidgeting with her hair. "I look a mess."

"You look fine to me."

"Well, make yourself at home. Dinner will be ready soon. Reuben, take him into the lobby where he can be more comfortable."

Stone pointed to a chair near the stove. "Can't I just sit there and watch? Hmm, that cornbread smells mighty good."

Juliette spun around quickly and grabbed at the stove's door. "The cornbread! I nearly forgot. Do you think it's too done?" she asked as she extended the hot pan toward him.

He looked at the heavily blackened edges with a lifted brow. "Naw. Just the way I like it. Well done."

"I wanted it to be perfect," she groaned with a scowl as she placed the hot pan on an iron trivet. "But it's ruined."

"Looks perfect to me."

"You're just saying that because you're a gentleman."

Stone took her hand in his. "I'm saying it because you fixed it for me, and I'm grateful. I'm sure it'll be fine. Don't fret yourself about it." He sniffed at the air. "Beans smell good."

She turned away and lifted the lid on the big pot. "They do smell good, don't they?"

Stone moved up beside her, took the long-handled spoon, and began to stir. "Ah, we may have a problem. These beans are kinda stuck to the bottom of the pot. Fire must be a mite hot." He lifted the spoon from the boiling mass and gazed at a wad of burnt beans.

She ran from the room with a shriek, her head in her hands.

Stone pulled the pot from the fire and dropped into the chair.

A few minutes later she returned, wearing a wan smile. "Well, do you still want to marry me, or is the wedding off?"

He touched the tip of her nose. "I didn't ask to marry you because of your cooking capabilities. I have America for that."

"Sorry about the beans and cornbread."

He picked up his plate and carried it to the table, where she'd put the hot pan. After carefully cutting a piece of cornbread from the area where it was blackest, he topped it with a massive scoop of the burnt beans. "America burns them all the time," he quipped with a broad smile. "They're exactly like I like them."

She reached for her own plate. "Liar."

"What about the rest of the family? Aren't they going to eat supper with us?"

"Not tonight. Caroline fed them earlier. I thought we needed a chance to talk—just the two of us. There are decisions to be made and things to discuss."

Stone took a forkful of beans and cornbread and ate them as though they were the best beans he'd ever tasted.

Juliette watched, then took a bite of her own. "They're awful!"

"I wouldn't exactly say awful."

"Well, I would!" She grabbed his plate and scraped the

contents into a small tub of food scraps. "I'll fix you a sandwich."

He watched as she sliced the bread and topped it with thick wedges of smoked pork, glad he wasn't going to have to eat that big plate of beans to appease her.

He took her hand in his when she brought the sandwiches to the table. Since he attended church regularly, he was sure she'd expect him to pray. "I think we need to get our relationship off to a proper start by thanking God for this food."

She bowed her head.

"Thank You, God, for this food—" He sneaked a peak at his companion, then added, "and for Juliette's willingness to share it with me. And all the other blessings You've poured out upon us. We bring Mary to Your attention and ask that You will make her well soon so she can attend our wedding. And—ah—I thank You that Juliette has agreed to become my wife. Amen."

She lifted misty eyes to his. "Amen," she echoed. "That was so sweet of you, to pray for my mother."

After they'd finished their meal and the table had been cleared, Stone asked, "How soon do you want to announce our engagement?"

"As soon as we're sure Mother is going to be all right."

For the next hour, the pair discussed their wedding plans, with Stone agreeing with everything Juliette said.

"Well," he began awkwardly when they'd finished, "thanks for supper. I'd best be gettin' on home. Guess I won't see you again until Sunday. That is, unless you need me for something, with your mother and father gone."

"I have plenty to do here, and hopefully we won't be needing you. But if we do, I'll send Reuben."

"Then, Sunday it is," he said with a tip of his hat as he backed out the door, nearly bumping into two incoming hotel guests. "At church. Save me a seat."

૨ð

Four days later, looking weary and tired, John Baker arrived home without Mary.

"How is she, Father?" Juliette asked with a worried frown.

"Better, I think. She went right to bed when we got there. She was tired from the trip, of course, but I think Doc was right. She needs uninterrupted rest. I wish I could've stayed with her, but I wanted to check on you children. How have things been going?"

"Mr. Piper—"

Juliette's hand clamped over Caroline's mouth. "It's my secret. Let me tell him."

Her younger sister stopped talking, despite the fact that she looked as though she was about to burst with the good news.

"I think you'd better sit down, Father. It's about the hotel."

John lowered himself onto the horsehair sofa and cupped his face with his hands. "Things look mighty bleak, and I apologize to you girls. I never thought I'd see the day I wouldn't be able to provide for my family. But it seems it's come to that. I can't even offer—"

Juliette dropped to her knees before him, pulled his hands from his face, and took them both in hers. "Father, you don't have to worry anymore. The hotel is yours! We won't have to move after all, and we've had every room rented since you left. I've been—"

John lifted his face and stared at his eldest daughter. "What are you talking about? What do you mean, the hotel is mine?"

She placed her hand over his affectionately. "The hotel belongs to you. Stone took care of it at the bank. The bill of sale has been signed, and your name is recorded as its sole owner!"

"Stone did that?" His face took on a deep frown. "But how? And why?" John closed his eyes and allowed his shoulders to slump. "He talked you into marrying him, didn't he? Because of me."

Juliette shook her head vigorously. "No! That's not the way it was! It was my decision!"

John squinted. "Oh, Daughter. No one should have to marry someone they don't love to save their family. He should never have forced this upon you."

Juliette pulled her hanky from her sleeve and wiped at her father's eyes. "Don't blame Stone. It *was* my decision. He did it for you, for all of us, and he's going to be a father to my baby. We'll never want for anything. It's going to be wonderful!"

"But, can you honestly say you love him, Juliette? You said you'd never marry a man you didn't love. Remember?"

She hesitated.

"Juliette, I've asked you a question."

"I—ah—I once heard that love isn't always a funny feeling in the pit of your stomach when the other person is around. It's an act of will. And Father, if any person deserves to be loved, it's Stone Piper. I'm hopeful I can learn to love him in time."

John took a deep breath and exhaled it slowly. "Is that going to be enough for you? This is a lifetime commitment."

"I can't honestly say. But I know Stone is a wonderful man. I've only recently realized it. And I have Andrew to consider. Marrying Stone will give my son things and opportunities I could never give him. What more could I ask of a man?"

"You could ask for love, like you had with David," he reminded her softly.

"A love like that may only come around once in a lifetime. All I could ever want is right in front of me, being handed to me by one of the finest, most thoughtful men in the community. Dare I wait to see if love happens in my life again?"

"You've resigned yourself to this, Daughter?"

"Yes, Father, I have. Stone and I are going to be married."

"You should've seen the supper she fixed for him while you were gone," Reuben cut in with an outright laugh as he came through the front door. "Burned both the beans *and* the cornbread. That man's crazy to marry her."

John's somber face took on a smile. "She burned them? Really?"

Juliette allowed a snicker to escape her lips. "Burned them something awful. I had to fix us sandwiches."

"But he still wants to marry her. Can you believe that?"

Juliette swatted at her brother. "Be quiet."

⁂

The night was still. Stone tossed and turned, unable to fall asleep despite the hard work he'd done all day. Deep in his bones, he felt an uneasiness that couldn't be explained. Even thoughts of his upcoming marriage and bringing his boys home couldn't soothe his restlessness.

Was that the sound of horses' hooves off in the distance? He sat up in bed and listened intently as the sound grew louder. *Who could be coming to Carson Creek Ranch this time of night? Well, whoever it is, I'll be ready for them.*

He pulled on his pants and shirt, grabbed his jacket and his rifle, and stepped out onto the porch as a band of men on horseback appeared in the faint streams of moonlight fanning their way across the yard. He squinted in the darkness, unable to make out the riders, his hand tightening on his trusty rifle.

"Halt!"

He immediately recognized Zach Nance's voice as the band came to a stop, the dust whipping up in a cloud about the horses' hooves. "What's wrong, Nance? What are you doing here this time of night?"

"Clint Norton rode into town and said a band of outlaws are robbing and torching settlers' homes up the creek from you. They've already burnt down Homer Bailey's place. We've got to stop them."

"Where's the sheriff? He know about this?"

Zach Nance shook his head. "He's taking care of trouble somewhere else. That's why we came for you."

"Give me a second." He rushed back into the house, pulled a second rifle and a revolver from a shelf, and filled a saddle-bag with ammunition before grabbing his leather vest from the peg.

Moses had heard the commotion and saddled Blackie by the time Stone rushed into the barn. "Take care of things, Moses," he shouted as he mounted the big horse. "Don't take any chances if those men come by here. Keep your gun handy."

Stone joined the men who'd already assembled when the alarm went out, and they moved toward the creek with Stone in the lead. "Anyone seriously hurt?"

"I'm afraid so. Bailey's dead. Don't know about his wife. Clint was pretty shaken up and didn't have many details. He was lucky to get away undetected."

Stone nodded. "What is it with men who think they can ride in and take the belongings good folks have worked a lifetime for?"

"Human nature, I guess."

"Sinful nature, I'd call it," Stone said with disgust. "Just like the Bible says."

"Couldn't agree more," a familiar voice sounded as one of the riders rode up to join the two men.

"John, that you?" Stone guided Blackie nearer the man. "I didn't know you were back. How's Mary?"

"Better."

They rode the rest of the way in silence until they neared the MacGregor house.

Stone turned toward his troops, lifted a hand, and tugged on the reins of his horse. "Gentlemen, we're getting close to where the outlaws were last spotted. When we get there, I think we'd best separate. Zach, you take four of the men and circle around to the north. I'll take four, and we'll ride along next to the creek. John, you come with me. You other three men go to the west with Jake Murdock. Everybody else, stay here on the south side. I'll give all of you time to get into your positions. Then, when you see me ride in, come at them from all four sides. Let's try to surprise them."

He cleared his throat and looked around at his ragtag group of volunteers. None of them knew much about fighting a gang of cutthroats, but he knew each one would do his very best. He just hoped no one would be injured. . .or worse yet, killed.

"From what Clint Norton told us, they're riding from north to south. He said they've already hit the Baileys', the Carters', and the Baxters' places. All three were on fire, and from the smell of things, so is the MacGregor house. We have no idea where any of the families are or if they're even alive. Keep an eye out for them; they may have escaped on foot and be in the woods somewhere."

"Smoke's getting stronger, Deputy Piper," Jake Murdock shouted from behind him.

"I know. We're getting close. Be careful. These outlaws are desperate and incredibly stupid to think they can get away with something like this. They'll probably shoot at anything that moves. More than likely, they've been drinking, and their brains aren't functioning too well. I don't want to have to take any of you men back to your family strapped across your horse's back. If the gang is still there, take cover. Don't be an open target."

His men nodded solemnly.

When Zach Nance and the other men broke off and headed toward the north, Stone and his group headed east, staying close to the edge of the creek. John rode directly behind him. The smoke became strong enough to gag them. As they rounded the top of a slight mound, they could see flames shooting into the sky.

Stone turned and told his men, "The family may still be in the house! Watch for them!"

In the north, he could see Zach Nance and those who rode with him. Jake Murdock and his men were to the west. Everyone was in place. He gave the signal, and they rode in.

It was difficult, despite the light from the burning home, to distinguish which men were theirs and which were the outlaws. Stone spotted Mrs. MacGregor and her three children huddled behind a broken-down wagon. "John, take them into the woods where they'll be safe! And stay with them!"

John shouted back, "I'll take them, but I'm coming back!"

"That's an order, Mr. Baker! I'll cover you. Go!"

Covering John, Stone watched until he was sure the MacGregor family was safely deposited in the woods, then rode in to Zach Nance's side as bullets whizzed through the air. "We found MacGregor's family! But he wasn't with them! Have you seen him yet?" he shouted above the noise.

"We think he's still inside, but I haven't been able to get near the house," the man shouted back. "They must've tied him up or taken him! I'm sure he'd have come out on his own by now!"

Stone blinked hard. "That, or he's dead. I'm going in after him."

"No!" Nance shouted with a wave of his hand. "It's not safe. You'll never make it! There're more of these guys than we thought!"

"Cover me!" Stone shouted back as he rode Blackie straight across the yard toward the burning cabin. As he leaped from the horse's back, he slapped him across the rump to send him on his way, then threw himself into the doorway of the burning house.

"MacGregor, are you here? Where are you?" he called out.

Nothing.

"MacGregor, can you hear me?" he shouted even louder, intent on finding the man.

Still, no answer.

Stone dropped to the floor and began to crawl around, searching with his hands through the smoke and flames. He was just about to give up when he heard a slight moan. Moving quickly toward the sound, he found Calvin MacGregor. His hands were tied behind his back, a deep gash crossed his arm, and he was nearly to the point of unconsciousness. "Hang on! I'll get you out of here!"

Stone cut the ropes and dragged the man to the door, then whistled for Blackie. The obedient horse darted back across the yard. "Good boy, Blackie!" He lifted the man and draped him across the saddle, hoping he'd stay put. Then, once more, he slapped the horse's rump. Stone took off toward the trees as a shot whizzed by his face, narrowly missing him. A second shot crackled and whizzed past him, this time grazing his forehead and causing him to lose hold of his gun as he dove for the shelter of the woodpile.

As Stone wiped away the blood from his face, he heard someone calling for help on the opposite side of the woodpile. John and one of the outlaws were struggling. The man had a headlock on John, with the tip of his knife pressing against John's throat.

Stone leaped into the air and thrust his body across the man, forcing him to release his hold on John.

"Get out of here!" Stone shouted at John as he fought to get the upper hand.

John hesitated. "It's my battle!"

"Go! That's an order!"

With Stone's attention momentarily diverted, the man seized the moment and rammed the knife's point deep into Stone's shoulder. Excruciating pain exploded in Stone's body. Blood gushed forth like an untamed river and soaked his shirt.

As the man scurried away, a second member of the gang flung himself on Stone, pinning him to the ground. In pain, but with anger as his catalyst, Stone wrapped his good arm tightly about the man's neck and squeezed, remembering what had happened to Bailey and the others.

"That's the man who shot and killed Homer Bailey!" John screamed out over the fracas. "He bragged about it!"

Stone stared at his assailant, then tightened his grip on the man's throat even more until he began to gasp for air.

As they struggled, the outlaw was able to pull one arm free. He poked his fat finger into Stone's eye. For a brief moment, Stone lessened his grip long enough for the outlaw to become the aggressor as the two wrestled on the ground.

He and the man were evenly matched, Stone realized all too quickly. With the wound in his shoulder, he feared he might end up the loser. But to him, losing his own life was better than losing John's. John's family needed him. Calling upon every ounce of strength he had left, Stone flipped the man over on his side and lay on top of him, hoping to be able to get in one good punch that would render the man helpless.

But as quick as a bolt of lightning, his assailant pulled a revolver from beneath his belt and pointed it at Stone's gut. "Die, Fool!"

Stone froze. Could he possibly move fast enough to get control of the gun before the man pulled the trigger? Or would this be the end of him? If he did nothing, the man would shoot him. He had nothing to lose. He had to take a final chance. Stone grabbed the gun's barrel. By sheer force and a will to live, he worked to turn it away from himself.

Boom!

The gun went off.

One man fell limply to the ground.

Dead.

Stone lay pinned to the cool ground, the outlaw draped across him. With one final burst of energy, he shoved the man's heavy body off and struggled to his feet, his head spinning.

"I've got you." John tugged Stone's good arm around his neck and dragged him to the safety of the trees where the MacGregor family huddled together. He placed Stone on the ground and tended to his wounded shoulder as best he could. "I need to get you to Doc Meeker. That knife went in pretty deep, and your head doesn't look much better."

"Can't go," Stone muttered almost incoherently as he fought against John's restraint and tried to stand. "Need to get my gu—" He fell back against his friend's chest.

"Hold your fire!" Zach Nance's voice boomed out loudly enough for everyone to hear. "We got them!"

Everything went silent except for the crackling sounds of the burning remains of the MacGregor home. The outlaws' robbing and killing spree had come to an end.

"It's over," John said with a deep sigh of relief as he leaned over Stone. "I'll look for your gun, then we can go home."

Stone sucked in a gasp of air. With great effort, he grasped at John's sleeve and again tried to pull himself up. "He's— he's dead, isn't he?"

"Yes, but he's the one who pulled the trigger. You were

only defending yourself. He would've killed you."

"I—never—never wanted him to die," Stone whispered faintly just before he lost consciousness.

❧

Juliette sat up in bed, wakened by the sound of horses' hooves thundering down Main Street. She grabbed her robe and ran down the stairs. By the time she reached the street, Zach Nance and some of the other men were pulling the outlaws off their horses, their hands tied behind their backs. Mr. Nance was shouting angrily at them and shoving them toward the general store. "Get Ward," he told the man called Smith. "We'll hold them in his store until we can get them to the calaboose."

She scoured the crowd for her father. At first, she couldn't spot him. Then she caught sight of him pulling a man from a horse, and the man's shirt was soaked with blood.

Her father's frightened voice echoed through the street. "Juliette, come quickly! Stone's been knifed!"

Juliette rushed to her father's side and assisted him in lowering Stone from Blackie's back. "Is he—"

"No, but he needs help. Go get Doc Meeker. Quick!"

"I'm here."

Juliette turned to find Doc Meeker, bag in hand, rushing to their side. "I heard the group riding into town and thought I might be needed. How bad is he?"

"Pretty bad, I'm afraid," John admitted as he pulled a big handkerchief from his pocket and wiped at Stone's brow. "Got knifed in the shoulder, and he's got a head wound too. The guy was aiming to kill him. He's lost a lot of blood."

"Can we get him into the hotel? I need light and water."

"Certainly." John motioned to Juliette. "Go on ahead, Girl. Light the lamps and put some water on to boil."

As much as she hated to leave Stone, she did as she was told. By the time she'd lit the lamps, several of the men were carrying him into the kitchen and placing him on the table. She hurriedly put the water on, then rushed to his side. "Will he be all right?"

"Don't know yet," Doc admitted as he lifted the edge of the bloody shirt from Stone's shoulder. "He's a pretty tough fellow."

She hurried to check on the water, then rushed back to his side. It frightened her to see Stone lying so still.

"I could use some clean rags," Doc was saying.

"I'll get them." Caroline moved quickly from her place on the stairway. "You stay with him, Juliette. He needs you."

Juliette nodded toward her sister appreciatively. She wanted to stay by his side. *Oh, dear God. I've lost one husband already. Not Stone too. Please spare him.*

Stone stirred slightly, opened wide the eye that wasn't nearly swollen shut from the gash, and stared at the ceiling.

Doc shook him gently. "Stone, it's Doc. Can you hear me?"

No response.

"Stone, look at me. You've been knifed. Do you remember?"

He gave a slight nod.

"You've lost a lot of blood, and you're probably feeling quite dizzy, am I right?"

The eye blinked several times.

"How many fingers am I holding up?"

Again the eye blinked, then a feeble voice answered, "Three, Doc. Plus your thumb."

Doc laughed. "I'd say he's going to be all right, just pretty weak for a few days, and we'll have to watch that wound."

Juliette cradled her throat with her hand and muffled a nervous laugh. Stone was going to recover.

Caroline entered with the rags Doc had requested.

"You suppose that water is hot by now?" Doc took the rags and began tearing them into strips.

"Yes, I'll get it." Juliette hurried off to the kitchen and returned with a pot of bubbling water, which she placed on the table beside Doc.

"Thanks. I'll need some assistance getting this bloody shirt off him. I've got to get that wound cleaned up."

Both Juliette and her father moved in to help. She tugged

on the sleeve while John steadied Stone's arm and Doc cut the shirt off his shoulder. Although Stone didn't make a sound, she knew he had to be in terrible pain, being shifted around like that.

"Take a rag and wash the blood off as close to his wound as you can, Juliette," Doc ordered as he rummaged through his bag.

She dipped a rag into the hot water, carefully wrung out the cloth, and tested the temperature before touching it to Stone's skin. He gave her a slight smile as she leaned over him and began to wipe away the blood. She'd never seen him without a shirt before. Although she'd been sure he would have well-developed muscles from his work as a rancher, she was surprised at the beauty of his physique and the even, golden color of his skin—no doubt from years of working out in the sun. She hadn't touched a man's skin like this since she'd lost David. It felt strange. Intimate. And although her father, Doc, and Caroline were in the room, she felt as if the two of them were sharing a private moment. As she gazed on this man of strength, she knew she would be safe living under his roof. He would do whatever was necessary to protect her and her baby, always.

Juliette grimaced each time the needle entered Stone's flesh as Doc stitched up the wound. Finally, after applying a thick, dark salve and bandaging the shoulder, Doc closed his bag. "I've done all I can do for him. He'll need to keep that sling on for a few days, and I'd prefer he stay at the hotel tonight. If he's doing all right, he can go back to his ranch tomorrow afternoon. That work, John?"

"Of course. I wouldn't have it any other way. And thanks, Doc. I owe this man my life."

"A lot of folks in this town could probably say the same thing." Doc picked up his bag. "Guess I won't have to worry about you, Stone. I can see you're in good hands," he said with a smile as he gestured toward Juliette. "I know you're in terrible pain. Have John fix you a toddy. That'll help."

John laughed. "Stone Piper, drink brandy? He won't touch it."

"If he hurts bad enough, he might," Doc answered with a grin.

Stone gave a slight flinch. "No, th–thanks. I'll tough it out."

"Suit yourself. That laudanum I gave you should help. I put a bottle on the table."

Stone lifted a hand toward Doc. "Isn't that stuff opium?"

"Oh, so you know your medicines, do you?"

Stone wrinkled his nose. "Think I'll pass on that too. Heard bad things about men having trouble giving that stuff up once they got on it."

Doc laughed. "Well, if you need it, it's there. Good night."

John closed the door and walked back to the sofa. "I'll sit up with him, Daughter. Go on to bed."

Juliette scooted closer to the sofa and put a hand on Stone's good shoulder. "Have you forgotten, Father? Stone is going to be my husband. I'll take care of him. Go on to bed. You need your sleep. I'll call you if I need you."

"But I—"

"You heard her, John," Stone inserted with a moan. "Juliette'll take care of me."

John shrugged, waved good night, and headed up the stairs.

Juliette lowered the lamp and pulled a chair up close beside the sofa. "Are you warm enough?"

"Yes. Don't worry about me."

"But you must hurt awfully bad. Will you be able to sleep?"

"I–I could, if I knew you were upstairs sleeping in your bed instead of down here watching over me," he whispered with effort.

She scooted her chair even closer. "I have no intention of leaving. I'm staying right beside you. You might need something."

"Like what? What could I need?"

She thought a moment. "Another blanket. Maybe a glass of water."

He gave a slight groan as he attempted to shift his position. "Or a soothing hand on my brow?"

"Even that."

He closed his eyes and relaxed a bit. "If I were Andrew, would you sing me a lullaby?"

"Possibly, if you were having trouble going to sleep."

"I'm having trouble."

"Well, let me see—" She leaned forward and began to sing very softly. "Sleep little baby, shut your eyes. Morning will come by and by. Angels will guard and care for you. Nobody loves you like I do."

"After you sing to him, what do you do?" he asked in barely audible words.

She stared at the man she knew had to be in dreadful pain as he lay unbelievably still on the sofa. "I cover him and kiss him good night."

His breathing settled into a rhythmic pattern, and once again, she was sure he had drifted off.

"I'm waiting," he said in a low murmur, "for my kiss."

"Thank you, Stone. For everything," she whispered softly before bending to plant a slight kiss on the cheek of this unselfish man. As she did, she remembered the testimonies she'd heard of his heroism, and she was suddenly overcome by deep emotion and thankful heart. Dove City's residents thought of him as a hero, and now so did she.

"You're my hero too," she said in a voice so soft she doubted he'd be able to hear it.

He opened one eye. "Your hero, huh? I kinda like the sound of that."

seven

Juliette dozed off during the night but woke each time Stone's breathing grew uneven, he moaned, or he'd shift his position. Although she couldn't make out the time on the wall clock in the semidarkness of the room, she knew it would soon be dawn.

Suddenly, Stone grabbed at her wrist and began making sounds like those of a whimpering child. She took his hand in hers and realized he was not awake but dreaming. He mumbled something almost incoherently at first, then the words became clearer. "Lucy, Lucy. I won't, I won't. Lucy—"

Juliette shook him gently, fearing he was having a nightmare about Lucy's death. "It's me. Juliette. You're dreaming."

He stopped thrashing about, and his body grew still as his eyes opened wide. "Di—did I say anything?" he whispered as he held tightly to her hand.

"Nothing I could understand," she answered, not wanting to upset him. "You're probably running a fever, that's all."

"You've been here at my side all night, haven't you?"

She stroked the good side of his forehead gently. "Yes. How are you feeling? How's the shoulder?"

He moved slightly. "Uggh. Sore."

"Your head looked pretty nasty too. How did that injury happen?"

Stone cringed as he lowered his shoulder back onto the pillow. "Shot grazed my head after I came out of MacGregor's cabin."

Fear coursed through her veins at the thought. "A shot came that close to your head? Oh, Stone. You could have been killed!"

"Yes, he could have," her father added as he came in with a

96

fresh glass of water. "Three times. Once by that shot. The second time by the man who knifed him. Then when that gun went off, it could've hit Stone as easily as it did its owner."

Amazed, she turned quickly back toward Stone. "What happened to that man?"

Her father answered for him. "He died."

Juliette let out a loud gasp. "I didn't know. Oh, Stone. I had no idea what you went through. He died? How awful you must feel."

"Juliette, that man tried to kill him," her father inserted quickly in his defense. "It was him or Stone. Stone tried to get the gun away from him, but the man pulled the trigger during their scuffle. There was nothing Stone could do. It wasn't his fault."

"Oh, I wasn't blaming Stone, I just—"

Stone clamped his eyes shut and gnawed at his lip. "I didn't mean for him to die. It just happened. I wish I could've prevented it. Maybe captured him instead of—"

"But you couldn't," Father interjected. "I witnessed the whole thing. The man's death was unavoidable. He pulled the trigger, not you."

Stone's fingers touched the cloth covering his shoulder. "But it happened nonetheless. His blood is on my hands."

"That's not so. Don't even think it!" John replied sharply. "If it weren't for you, even more lives would've been lost. Ask anyone who was there last night. Ask Zach Nance. Ask MacGregor. Ask me!"

"They all said you were a hero," Juliette added proudly. "I heard them."

"Don't feel much like a hero."

"Well, you are one." John placed the glass on the table. "I'm taking over now, Juliette. Go upstairs and get some sleep. Stone is my responsibility now."

"No, he's mine. I'll take—"

"Do what your father says, Juliette. Andrew will be waking up before long. You'll need to be rested. Go on up to bed."

Reluctantly, she nodded. "Oh, all right, but first I need to check the covering on your wound." She carefully removed the clean dressing Doc Meeker had placed on his shoulder. It was only slightly damp with blood and the watery substance that had seeped from his wound. The sight of his stitched-up flesh made her light-headed, but she wouldn't let on.

"How's it look?" he asked through gritted teeth.

She knew he'd never admit to how much pain he was in. "Well, I'm not exactly sure how it should look, but I can tell it needs a clean wrapping. I'll try not to hurt you."

"You won't hurt me," he assured her as his fists clenched at his sides.

Juliette held her breath as she pulled the cloth from the cut, which, in her opinion, was looking quite nasty. She dabbed the area around the wound with a dampened cloth, wiping it as clean as possible without removing the salve or hurting him, then applied a fresh one. "There, that should hold until Doc Meeker comes by. I'm sure he'll do a much better job." She straightened the comforter and tucked it around his body.

"But he's not as pretty as you are," he said, flinching and letting out his breath. "Thanks. Now do as your father says. Get some sleep."

"Well, if you're sure—"

"I'm sure." He reached out a hand and touched hers. "I wouldn't have made it through the night without you. Thanks."

Juliette felt herself blushing. "I didn't do anything."

"You were here. That's what counts."

She patted his good shoulder, kissed her father's cheek, and headed up the stairs with a backward glance toward the sofa. *Yes, he's going to make a fine husband.*

❧

Stone shifted his position with a groan and turned toward John. "You never told me about Mary, other than she was getting better."

"I'll be bringing her back home soon, I hope," John said with a slight smile curling at his lips. "Maybe in another couple weeks. If she continues to improve, she'll be home in plenty of time for your wedding."

Stone smiled back. "Oh, so you've heard."

"I heard. Juliette told me all about it. The last things I expected to be told when I came home were that the bill of sale for the hotel had my name on it and that my daughter was making wedding plans. How can I ever thank you?"

"You just did. Besides, I'm getting a wife out of this deal."

John's smile disappeared, and his face became somber. "You shouldn't have done it. You know she doesn't love you—not like a woman should love the man she intends to marry."

"I know," Stone conceded with a sigh. "She's a fine woman, but I don't love her either. Never will—not in that way. I promised Lucy I'd never love another woman, and I intend to keep my promise."

"So—you won't—ah—"

Stone smiled. "No, I won't consummate the marriage. You don't have to worry about that. Juliette and I have an agreement. We understand each other. We're going to get along just fine. I promise you, John; I'll take care of her and that son of hers as if they were my own."

"You still gonna be my friend now that I'm gonna be your father-in-law?"

"Of course," Stone assured him. "Just don't go pushing me around."

"I have one question: She'd made it perfectly clear she was not going to marry you. How'd you get her to go through with it?"

Stone grinned. "I didn't. She asked *me* to marry her."

❧

Stone was wide-awake, propped up on a pillow against the arm of the sofa, when Juliette and Andrew came down the stairs about nine. "Well, there's my little man," he said when he saw Andrew cuddled in her arms. "You didn't keep your mother awake, did you?"

Juliette handed the baby to her father and hurried to Stone's side. "Did you make it through the rest of the night all right?"

"Even without the brandy," her father said with a chuckle. "Although I know he was in more pain than he'd let on. This is one tough man."

Despite Stone's objection, she pulled back the bandage from his shoulder with a gasp. "It's still bleeding a bit. You'd better let me put on a fresh dressing."

"Not necessary. Really. Doc'll do it later."

She ignored him and set about removing the soiled cloths.

He cringed and his eyes widened.

"You are hurting. Oh, Stone—"

"A bit," he confessed as he shifted slightly. "Guess a certain amount of pain goes with the territory. It's better'n being dead, I reckon."

"Don't say that." She gave him a slight slap on his good shoulder. "From what Father and Mr. Nance said, you could've easily died last night, several different times."

"They were exaggerating."

Father stepped forward. "No, Stone. We weren't. You're lucky to be alive. So are we. If it weren't for you—"

"If I hadn't stepped in, you would have handled that man without me."

"That's not so! He was nearly twice my size. I didn't have a chance. It'd have been me you'd have been burying, not him."

Stone shrugged his good shoulder. "Well, I guess that's something we'll never know. I say you would've handled him without me." His face took on a look of defeat. "At least you didn't cause a man to die."

Her father shook his head. "How many times do I have to tell you? *He* was the one who pulled the trigger, not you. The gun was in *his* hand. You can't blame yourself for his death. If he and the rest of those no-good men hadn't been out robbing, killing, and setting homes on fire, you'd have been out at your ranch, safe and sound. They brought it upon themselves. Think about what they did to those families."

"I'm not so sure—"

"Well, I am," Father stated firmly. "Now, let's have no more of this foolish talk."

"Is that cut on your head paining you much?" Juliette asked as she finished taking care of his shoulder.

Stone's hand rose to the spot. "Naw, I'd forgotten all about it."

The front door of the hotel opened. Two adults and three children stepped inside.

"Well, good morning, MacGregor family. You're out and about early." Her father moved to shake Mr. MacGregor's hand. "Welcome."

The entire family nodded, then moved directly to stand before the wounded man on the sofa.

"Heard you was spending the night here at the hotel, Stone," Mr. MacGregor began. "Me and the missus and my children want to thank you for what you did for us."

Mrs. MacGregor dropped to her knees in front of Stone, tears bursting from her eyes as she looked at him. "Our home can be replaced, but if you hadn't gone into that burning house, Calvin wouldn't be here."

Calvin knelt down and put an arm about her shoulders, his own eyes misting over. "If you hadn't drawn attention to yourself while John led my family to the safety of the trees, I might've—"

Stone blushed and turned his head away. "Aw, come on, you two. Stop it. You know you'd have done the same thing—"

Mr. MacGregor shook his head. "Stone, don't try to act like what you did was nothing. You're a hero, not only to our family but to the entire community."

Juliette listened to the grateful family from her place next to Stone. Hearing of his bravery from the McGregors made the danger seem even more real than it had sounded the night before. He *was* a hero.

"Not one word," Stone cautioned Juliette when they were alone. "I don't want to hear anymore about that hero stuff."

She went back to her task of cleaning his wound and putting fresh padding on the area where the bowie knife had done its work and on his head. "But you are—"

He held a palm up toward her. "I said, no more!"

"No more what?" Doc Meeker asked as he pushed open the door and made his way to his patient's side.

"That hero stuff. I don't like it and I don't deserve it," Stone explained as Doc pulled up a chair and sat down beside him.

"Oh, I see. You're a bit modest, eh?"

Juliette stepped back with a slight snicker as she let Doc take over. "Modest? Stone?"

"Well, you'd better get used to the title. Seems everyone I've met on the street this morning is calling you a hero." Doc pulled the cloth off the deep wound. "Looks pretty good, considering."

"Considering?" Juliette repeated as she leaned in for a better look.

"Considering the man was out to kill him instead of wound him," Doc reminded both of them as he inspected the wound.

Hearing Doc's words suddenly made her sick to her stomach. The wound *was* meant to kill Stone. If he hadn't been able to overpower the man, like her father had said— A tremor coursed through her body, and her knees felt weak.

Stone flinched as Doc poured a solution of some kind onto a cloth and applied it to his shoulder.

"Burn a bit?"

"Whew! What is that stuff? Liquid fire?"

Doc let out a chuckle. "Almost, but it'll help start the healing. If I let you go home today, you have to promise me you'll have America dab some of that on each time she changes the bandages. I mean *each* time, not just once in awhile. Understand? Wouldn't hurt to put some on that cut on your head too, if you're man enough to take it."

"You mean I can go home now?" Stone asked with an anxious look toward the woman who'd been taking care of him.

Doc nodded. "Yep. No better place to rest and recover than in your own bed."

❧

Reuben tugged on the reins, and the buggy came to a stop in

front of Stone's home. America opened the door wide and motioned to Juliette. "Hurry on in here! That wind's mighty chilly. We don't want that baby takin' no cold."

Juliette hurried in and found Stone sitting in a chair by the woodstove, looking much more fit than she'd expected.

He grinned and held out his hand. "Thought you'd never get here."

"I'm here now." She took off her cape, pulled the blanket off Andrew, and slipped into a chair beside the man she was going to marry. "How are you? How's the shoulder? Are you feeling any better? Let me see your head."

He held up his hand. "Whoa, Woman. One question at a time. I'm doing just fine. And, yes, I'm feeling much better, especially now that you're here. He pushed the hair back off his forehead with his good hand. "The bullet only grazed my head. See? It's healing nicely." He reached out and took Andrew's pudgy hand in his. "And how is this little man? He's really growing, isn't he?" He let loose of Andrew's hand and reached for hers. "How are you? I've missed you."

She allowed a weary sigh to escape her lips. "I'm doing all right, I guess. With Mother gone, it's been pretty difficult at the hotel these past few days. I never realized how much she did. Father is so lonely without her."

"Does he have any idea when she'll be ready to come home?"

She poured a fresh glass of water and handed it to him. "Yes, he does, and it's good news. While Gordon Haynes was in Conner's Corner visiting his aunt, he looked in on Mother. She said to tell Father she was feeling rested and much better. Her aunts and Molly have been taking care of the twins for her, and she's ready to come home anytime he can come and get her."

"Does this mean—"

She nodded, her face aglow with joy as she thought of their upcoming marriage. "Yes, we can set a date for our wedding. When shall it be?"

He grinned and shrugged, wincing a bit. "I'm ready. How

soon can *you* be ready?"

She thought for a moment. "One month. Is that too soon?"

"Not for me. How about you?"

"Where shall we have it? If we have it on a Sunday afternoon, we could have it at the saloon."

"The saloon will be too small if we invite as many folks as we said." He thought for a moment. "How about the mission?"

She clapped her hands together as her smile broadened. "Oh, what a good idea! That'll be a lovely place for a wedding. Maybe four weeks from this Saturday? In the early afternoon?"

"Perfect." He squeezed her hand. "I'll write my sister and tell her to have the boys here by then."

"Oh, I do hope they'll be able to come early. I'm so anxious to meet them."

"You're going to be my wife now. I want you to purchase anything you want on my account at Thomas Ward's store. That means anything, Juliette." He grinned sheepishly. "From shoes for Andrew to any personal items you need for yourself. Get anything you need to make our wedding the biggest and best Dove City has ever seen."

"And you'll wear a black coat and a pleated white shirt?"

"If you want me to, I will."

"And Caroline will be my bridesmaid."

"Of course, John will walk you down the aisle."

"Let's have cake and cider at our reception."

"We'll invite everyone we know." He braced his arm on the chair back with a groan. "But promise me one thing, Juliette."

"Of course. What?"

"Since you haven't been a widow very long, I understand why you have to wear those dark dresses; but do you think maybe your wedding dress could be that pretty mauve color? Or maybe dark blue?"

She smiled at his request. "I think that's a reasonable request. Which do you prefer?"

"Green."

She threw back her head with a giggle. "Green? I thought you said mauve or dark blue."

"I like green better. I just didn't know if it was proper."

"How about dark green? About the color of the oak leaves?"

He grinned. "That'd be nice."

"Then green it is. I like green too."

"Juliette?"

"Yes."

"Why don't you have that dressmaker, Lettie Farnes, make your wedding dress? I've heard tell she does good work. Maybe have her make you a couple of new dresses to wear around the house after we're married. Something more colorful than those black and gray things you've been wearing."

She gave him a mischievous smile. "You don't like my black and gray dresses?"

"Ah—sure I do," he said, obviously fumbling for words. "You look pretty in them, but I think it'd be nice for the boys to see you in color. That's all. What do you think?"

She laughed. "I think you're absolutely right. I'll drop by and talk it over with Lettie as soon as we announce our engagement."

"You've made me so happy, Juliette. I know my—ouch!"

"Stone! You're hurting. Why didn't you tell me?"

America pointed her finger at her boss as she came in from the kitchen. "Ya better stretch yourself out on that daybed for awhile. I'm gonna go put some extra pillows on it so you'll be comfortable."

"Yes, Stone, please do as America says," Juliette told him with great concern. Then smiling, she added, "I'd hate to have to help you down the aisle at our wedding."

"Whatever you ladies say." Wincing again, he struggled to his feet. "I've gotta get this wing of mine healed so I can carry you across the threshold." He reached for his bride-to-be's hand. "I can hardly wait for you to move in. It's going to be nice having you and the baby here in this house. I've been so lonely since—"

"Since Lucy died? That's the way I felt when I lost David. Especially when I'd go to bed at night. At times, I thought I'd die from the loneliness."

He took on a serious expression. "We're going to be a family soon. But I want you to know, once you're moved in, you can be assured of your privacy. I will never come into your room uninvited. As we've agreed, we won't—"

She put a finger to his lips. "I understand, and it's good to know you don't expect me to—" She gulped awkwardly. "Either."

"This is going to be your home as well as mine, you know. I want you to make any changes you'd like. Anywhere, except—"

She frowned. "Except where?"

"Never mind."

She confronted him directly. "No, let it out. I want to know exactly what you were about to say. No secrets."

He sucked in a deep breath. "Except the room I keep locked."

"That storeroom?" She could tell he was uncomfortable talking about it. Why would an old storeroom be such a problem?

"Yes, the storeroom. I don't want you going in there."

"But you said it was filled with things you should probably throw away. Maybe I can help you clean it out."

He grabbed her tightly by the wrist, and she pulled back in surprise. "No. Stay out of that room. Don't ever go in there."

"I won't!" she agreed, wondering why the mere mention of a simple storage room would make this peaceful man behave in such a strange, aggressive way.

He released his grip and leaned back against the pillow, his hand covering his eyes. "I'm sorry. I don't know what got into me. I must be more unnerved by my injuries than I thought. I didn't mean to upset you."

"I'm—I'm not upset. Just surprised," she explained, masking her concern. "I didn't know the old storage room was that important to you. I'll keep my distance from it, if that'll keep you happy."

Stone extended his hand. "Don't be mad at me, please."

"I'm not, honest I'm not. With all you've gone through—"

"That doesn't give me the right to take it out on you. There's never an excuse for anger, especially when the other person has done nothing to provoke that anger."

"Really, I understand." She took his hand in hers and gave it a slight squeeze. "I've got to be going now. I promised Caroline I'd help with supper."

He went from a frown to a grin. "Four weeks from Saturday?"

"Yes," she said as she gazed into his tired eyes. "Four weeks from Saturday."

"Can we announce our engagement at church this Sunday?"

"Yes, let's, if you feel like going. Everyone will be surprised."

"They're going to wonder how an old geezer like me could snag such a beautiful young woman."

Juliette felt a flush rise to her cheeks at his compliment. "Let them wonder. It'll be our secret."

"Does that mean you don't want me to tell them *you* asked *me* to marry *you?*"

❧

The time passed quickly as Juliette bustled about each day, preparing for their wedding. Finally the big day arrived.

"Wake up, Sleepyhead. It's your wedding day." Caroline giggled as she pulled the covers off her sister.

Juliette sat up with a start. She'd lain awake most of the night worrying about last-minute details, going over them one-by-one in her mind until she felt completely worn out. "What time is it?"

"Nearly eight," Caroline answered with a shake of her finger as she turned and moved into the hall. "You'd better hurry if you plan to make it to your wedding on time."

Juliette whizzed through the morning, packing a few final things for their move to Stone's, spending time with each of her siblings, and saying her good-byes. She knelt at her mother's side just before going to her room to dress for her wedding. "I want you to know how much I love you, Mother. What a wonderful example you and Father have been to me. While Stone and I are not marrying because we love each other, I do plan to use your example to create a happy home for our new family."

"Then listen carefully, Juliette. What you're about to hear is the most important advice I can give you." Her mother kissed her cheek, then wrapped Juliette in her frail arms. "Love God with all your heart and keep His commandments. Put God first in your life, your husband second, your children next, and yourself last."

Startled by her words, Juliette pulled back and stared into her mother's big brown eyes. "Put Stone above Andrew? When I don't love him?"

Her mother nodded. "Yes, put him above Andrew. He's going to be your husband, Juliette. In some countries, parents pick their children's spouses. Couples learn to love each other after they're married. You can do the same thing, if you try. If you really want to. Stone is a good man, one of the best. See that you honor him."

Juliette thought long and hard about her mother's words as she readied herself for her walk down the aisle. The advice sounded good, but would she be able to do it?

❧

John and his prospective son-in-law stood at the front of the great room in the mission house.

"Nervous?" John asked as he pulled out his timepiece for the fifth time.

"Me? Nervous?" Stone fingered at the tight, black string tie. "Think she'll go through with it? She won't back out?"

John shook his head. "Not a chance. The two of us had quite a talk last night. She's determined to marry you. By the way, you're looking good in that black suit and white pleated shirt. Never seen your hair slicked down like that."

"Think Juliette will like it?"

"She'd better. She's gonna be stuck with you for a lifetime. Your sister get here all right?"

Stone smiled as he nodded. "Yes, late yesterday. I can't

believe how my boys have grown. Gonna take them awhile to get used to having their old dad around again."

"Well, don't worry about it. Between the two of you and Andrew, they'll soon warm up and be calling your place home." He checked his timepiece again. "In five minutes, I'm going to walk my daughter down the aisle. Think you can make it on your own, or do you need Reuben to hold you up?"

Stone offered a nervous chuckle. "Never fear, John. I can make it. You know I'll be good to your daughter, don't you?"

John shook his friend's hand. "I'm counting on it. May God be with you both."

❧

Juliette blinked back tears of happiness as the double doors at the back of the big room opened and the pianist began to play. She glanced down at her dress, smiling at the lovely color—green, the color of oak leaves—as she held on to the arm of her beaming father. It was her wedding day, and she was happier than she'd ever expected she could be.

How generous Stone had been when he'd told her to purchase anything she'd need to make their wedding the biggest and best Dove City had ever seen. She moved slowly down the aisle, passing chairs filled with family and friends, her gaze fixed on her husband-to-be. Her heart pounded loudly within her, so loudly she was sure those seated nearest the aisle could hear it. But she didn't care. This was her wedding day.

The sight of so many people and the sounds of the music from the piano made her giddy. She wanted to laugh out loud, to tell everyone how happy she was. *Could I actually be falling in love with this man like my mother said?*

As she approached the first row of chairs, she pulled away from her father's grasp, bent, and kissed her mother's cheek. "I love you, Mother," she whispered before smiling at her precious Andrew, who was tugging at his grandmother's beads.

Her mother smiled up at her. "I love you, Juliette, my baby girl, my dear one. God be with you. And don't forget what I said."

Juliette proudly took her father's arm. Again, the two of them proceeded down the aisle to stand beside Stone, with her father between them and Caroline at her side.

Pastor Tyson opened his Bible and the ceremony began. "Who gives this woman to be married to this man?"

Father took Juliette's hand and placed it in Stone's. "Her mother and I do."

⚘

Stone wrapped his fingers around Juliette's delicate hand and grasped it tightly as he gazed into her eyes, but it was not Juliette he was seeing. It was Lucy. His heart broke, and he found himself pressing back tears as he remembered a wedding of seven long years ago.

After the pastor read from the Bible and explained what God's Word had to say about marriage, he challenged the couple to live for each other and for Christ. But Stone's thoughts had wandered to another time, another place.

"Stone?" Pastor Tyson whispered. "Are you listening?"

Stone straightened and took a deep, cleansing breath. "Yes, sorry. I–I'm listening."

⚘

Juliette watched as Stone seemed to have a battle going on within himself as he struggled for words. She wondered if he was having doubts or experiencing the same last-minute jitters that had plagued her all day. But the smile he sent her way and the squeeze she felt on her hand assured her nothing was wrong.

"Do you, Juliette Baker Martin, take Stone Jason Piper to be your lawfully wedded husband?"

She turned to the man standing beside her, so handsome in his black coat and white shirt, with his hair slicked down the way she liked it. "I do."

"Do you, Stone Jason Piper, take Juliette Baker Martin to be your lawfully wedded wife?"

Stone paused.

Juliette felt herself gasp. What if he didn't answer? Or said no?

Pastor Tyson seemed agitated by his delay. "Stone? Do you?"

She watched as Stone took a deep breath, then let it out slowly as he stared into her eyes, almost as if he didn't see her at all.

She squeezed his hand and waited as a lump rose in her throat. Was their marriage going to be over even before it began?

"I, ah—I do," he whispered softly.

"Speak up, Stone. I think your friends and family would like to hear you." Pastor Tyson smiled nervously toward their audience.

Stone blinked, then opened his eyes wide. "I do!" he stated firmly. "I do take this woman as my wife."

Juliette breathed out a quick sigh, as did the pastor.

Pastor Tyson placed his hand over theirs as they cupped them over the family Bible. "By the power of God, and in His sight, I now pronounce you husband and wife. What God hath joined together, let not man put asunder. You may kiss the bride."

The newly united couple stood gaping awkwardly at one another. Stone glanced around with a nervous expression, his free hand fidgeting with his string tie. Finally he bent and gently kissed Juliette's cheek.

"You're married now. Kiss your bride properly," Pastor Tyson whispered with a grin.

Juliette lifted her face toward Stone's. She realized, if Stone took the pastor's instructions to heart, this would be the first time he'd ever kissed her.

Stone turned to Pastor Tyson, his face flushed, and whispered back, "I'd prefer giving Juliette our first kiss as husband and wife in private, if it's all the same to you."

Pastor Tyson nodded his agreement, signaled the pianist, and the "Wedding March" began.

Stone grabbed his wife's hand, and they bolted back up the aisle and through the double doors.

"Sorry," he whispered after they'd reached the privacy of the foyer. "I just couldn't bring myself to kiss you in front of all those people. It just—well, you knows. We've—I've—I've never kissed you before. Somehow it didn't seem proper to have our first kiss in front of an audience."

She smiled. "I know. It felt that way for me too."

"None of them, except your family, know why we really got married. I'd just as soon keep it that way, if that's agreeable."

She managed to whisper a quick yes as the many well-wishers crowded into the foyer to congratulate the happy couple.

When all hands had been shaken and everyone had gathered around them, Juliette climbed up to the fifth step of the lovely oak stairway, turned, and tossed her bouquet over her shoulder. It fell into Caroline's hands.

Stone laughed as he whispered in her ear, "Ah, Caroline caught your bouquet. One of these days, maybe you'll have some little nieces around to pamper."

Juliette sent a quick glance over the crowd. "Which reminds me. Where is your sister? I haven't met her or your boys yet. I've been looking for them."

He quit smiling. "She had a headache. I sent her and the boys on home with Moses. You'll meet them later."

His reaction upset her, although she didn't know why. It did seem odd that he wouldn't at least introduce his children and his sister to her before sending them away; but if his sister hadn't been feeling well and the boys were tired and cranky from their trip, she'd just have to wait. There'd be plenty of time for that later. For now, they'd enjoy the company of their neighbors and friends.

"Got yourself a beautiful woman for a bride, you ugly old man," Doc Meeker teased as he shook their hands. "Don't strain that shoulder on your wedding night."

Juliette flashed a look of surprise at Stone.

"Don't worry about that, Doc. I've married me a lady. I intend to treat her as such."

She appreciated his evasive answer and gave him a look of approval.

"Well, I'd say Juliette got herself a fine gentleman. You leave this nice young couple alone now, do you hear me?" Mrs. Meeker told her husband as she pushed him toward the refreshment table.

"Sorry," Stone whispered in his bride's ear.

"It's all right. They meant well," she mumbled back as she turned to greet their next guest with a smile.

"I'm so happy for you and Stone," Ethel Benningfield told her as she smiled back. Then, leaning forward, she whispered, "I've been watching you since that day we spoke in the lobby of your parents' hotel. You've blossomed into a fine Christian woman. I can see the change in you, and I'm sure our Lord is pleased."

Juliette's heart was touched by her words. "He's brought our family through some real trials lately, but I've become much closer to Him through it all. Without God to turn to, I don't think any of us could have made it. But He answered our prayers. Mother is feeling much better. Father was able to purchase the hotel—"

"And you're marrying a fine, upstanding Christian man. My, but God has been good to you. Just keep your eyes on Him, and you two will do fine."

Juliette bent and kissed the woman's cheek. "I want you to know I appreciated your advice about my parents. Because of you, I'm learning to think twice before speaking." She leaned close so no one else could hear, then whispered in the woman's ear. "I still have trouble with my mouth. Words still seem to slip out when they shouldn't. Please pray for me. At times, I still have trouble with my temper too."

"I have been praying for you and will continue to do so." Ethel reached out and gave Juliette's hand a squeeze. "If you ever need someone to talk to, Dear, I'm always available."

Juliette watched as the woman walked away, remembering their prior conversation. Somehow, to her, it almost seemed that conversation had been a turning point in her life.

By three o'clock the cake and cider on the reception table had been enjoyed, and America and Caroline started cleaning up the wedding mess.

Juliette handed Stone the valise with the few remaining things she'd need in her new home. She'd prepared before leaving her father's house this morning. The rest of her belongings, along with Andrew's, had been taken to Carson Creek Ranch the day before. They were waiting for her in the room she'd occupy. "I'm ready."

"Where's Andrew?"

"Father will bring him out later. He was getting cranky."

Stone took her hand, and they headed for their buggy, which Moses had left parked by the door. The crowd of well-wishers cheered wildly when Juliette and Stone stepped hand-in-hand out of the mission.

After he waved, Stone gently lifted his new bride into the buggy, then climbed in beside her and took the reins.

Juliette snuggled close beside him, thinking that was what all new brides would do. But she didn't feel like a new bride. She felt like a traitor. They were deceiving all their friends.

Stone seemed to feel the same way. He leaned awkwardly toward her before whipping the reins and starting the horses toward home. "Guess we've gone and done it, Juliette."

"Yes, I suppose we have. Are you sorry?"

He leaned toward her, planting a kiss on her forehead. "Not one bit."

"Neither am I."

☙

There was no one to greet them when they reached the ranch. America had stayed behind to help Caroline clean up and put the mission house back in order. Moses had gone back after her. Juliette had been sure Alice, Stone's sister, would meet them at the door with open arms, but she didn't.

Her new husband assisted her as she exited the buggy, then whisked her up in his arms and held her close.

"Are you sure you should be doing this? With your shoulder?" she asked, genuinely concerned, knowing lifting her must be causing him a great deal of pain.

"I may not be the husband you wanted, Juliette, but I am going to carry you over the threshold like a proper husband would."

She wrapped her arms about his neck. "Just be careful, please. I wouldn't want you to hurt yourself because of me."

"I'm almost as good as new. Let me worry about that." He climbed the steps easily and pushed open the door before ceremoniously stepping across the threshold and depositing her on the other side. There, sitting on three chairs lined up in a row, were Alice, his oldest son, Eric, and a darling boy with tightly curled dark hair who had to be Will.

Juliette hurried to them, her hands extended. "Hello! I've been so eager to meet you. I'm Juliette. You must be Will. Eric, you look just as I thought you would. And you have to be Stone's wonderful sister, Alice."

The woman reached out her hand with a warm smile. "Hello, Juliette. It's nice to meet you too. Stone has told me so much about you and your wonderful family."

The older boy, Eric, stood. "Nice to meet you, Miss—"

Juliette hurried to his rescue. "Why don't you call me Juliette for now? Would that be all right with you?"

The child smiled, obviously relieved. "Uh huh."

She tousled the smaller boy's curly hair. "Will, you have no idea how excited I've been to meet you. I have a son too, only he's not as big as you are. I think you two will get along just fine. He'll be here before long, and you can get acquainted."

The boy didn't say a word, just stared at her with big, blue eyes topped with long curly lashes like his father's.

"Sorry I didn't get to meet you before the wedding, but we were a mite tired when we got in yesterday," Alice told her.

Juliette pulled up a chair and sat down beside the woman. "I was looking forward to meeting you. I'd hoped we could spend some time together before the wedding. I have so many questions for you because I want to make the boys feel at home. I want to know about their favorite foods, what games they like—all sorts of things like that. I hope you're going to stay long enough to tell me everything before you have to go back to St. Joseph."

Alice gestured toward the two boys. "Those are fine children—obedient, thoughtful, and very responsible. Eric looks after Will—"

Stone stepped in, breaking into her sentence before she could finish it. "She has to go back tomorrow. I've arranged transportation for her."

"Oh, no!" Juliette grabbed Alice's hand. "You can't leave so soon. I'm sure it would be much better for the boys if you were able to stay a few weeks—at least until they get used to me and their new surroundings."

"Impossible," Stone answered for his sister. "She has to get back to St. Joseph."

"But since you're not feeling well—" Juliette began.

Alice seemed confused. "Me, not feeling well? I'm fit as a fiddle. Whatever gave you that idea?"

"Your headache? The reason you couldn't stay for the reception. Is it gone now?"

Alice looked surprised. "I don't know what you're talking about. I haven't had a headache in years."

"She was tired from the trip. I guess I just supposed she had a headache," Stone explained awkwardly.

"Well, I didn't! I feel fine. I brought the boys back to the ranch before the reception because Stone wanted me to."

Juliette flashed a questioning look toward her husband, which he ignored as he extended his hand toward her.

"Come with me, Juliette. I want you to see what America and I have done to your room, and I'm sure you'll want to get out of that wedding gown and into something more comfortable."

Juliette refused his hand and stepped away from him. "I'd rather visit with Alice since she's leaving so soon."

"Come, Juliette," he said in a firm voice that irritated her. He was her new husband, but he had no right to make her decisions for her. "I said I want to show you your room. Now."

She offered Alice a feeble smile, then followed him down the hallway. As soon as she was sure they were far enough away that his sister couldn't hear them, she turned to him with a glare. "Don't you ever do that to me again! I don't appreciate being ordered around."

"I–I only wanted to show you your room. Don't you like it?" He gestured around the newly arranged room. "America put your things in the chest, and I moved this rocker in so you could rock Andrew."

"Stone, this is all well and good, and I appreciate it. But what I'm interested in right now is spending time with your sister and your boys before Father brings Andrew." She pushed him toward the door. "Now, give me some privacy, I want to change my clothes."

He moved awkwardly out the door, gently closing it behind him.

Within a matter of minutes, she was back in the living room, dressed in a calico frock. "Now, let's visit," she told their houseguests. She turned to the oldest boy. "Eric, tell me about your trip. Did you see any buffalo on the way?"

His eyes filled with enthusiasm. "Yes, Ma'am, a lot of them. Some coyotes too."

She leaned over and took Will's hand. "Did you see any buffalo or coyotes?"

The boy just stared at her.

"Will, did you see any buffalo?" she asked again, this time impatiently dropping to one knee in front of the lad.

Again, he simply stared at her without answering.

Alice shot a sudden look at Stone that Juliette couldn't interpret.

"Will," she said firmly, looking directly into the boy's face. "Did you see any buffalo?"

"He can't hear you, Juliette," Stone finally said, coming to stand by the boy. He's nearly deaf."

eight

Juliette felt faint. "Deaf?"

"Yes," Stone confessed in a nearly inaudible voice.

"How—how long has he been deaf?"

He shut his eyes, letting out a long sigh. "Si–since birth."

Juliette rose and beat her fists on his chest. "And you didn't tell me? Is this why Alice and the boys didn't arrive until just before the wedding? So I wouldn't know about this until after we were married?"

"I–I was afraid you wouldn't marry me."

"Because of Will's deafness? I'm not that kind of person!"

"I'm sure he thought he'd lose you, Juliette," Alice interceded in her brother's behalf. "Most women wouldn't want to take on a child with a hearing problem."

Stone nodded as if echoing his sister's comment. "Alice is right. That's exactly what I thought."

Alice stood and motioned to the boys to come to her. "Why don't I take the boys in the kitchen. I'm sure America can find something for them—a glass of milk or something."

Juliette searched her heart as she watched them go. The last thing she'd want to do was hurt those innocent little boys. Toning her voice down a bit, she continued. "I would've wanted some answers from you, Stone, and from Alice, since she's the one who has been caring for him. But I think I would have said yes. After all, you accepted Andrew and me with very little knowledge about us."

"I—ah, couldn't take that chance, Juliette. Before I could bring them home, I had to know I had a woman committed to help me with my boys. I knew I'd have a difficult time convincing any woman to take on the added responsibility of a deaf child."

What she wanted to do was scream at him; but for the sake of his children, she restrained herself and kept her voice on an even keel. "So you decided to trick me into it by keeping this a secret until after I'd married you? What kind of a man would do that? Are there any other surprises I should know about?"

"I didn't—"

"That's absolutely right. You didn't do right by me, Stone Piper!" She fell down onto the chair with a thud, frowning and crossing her arms. "Do you honestly think it was fair? To lie to me?"

"I didn't exactly lie, I—"

"No, you just didn't tell me the truth! Is that supposed to make it better?"

"I'm sure he meant no harm, Juliette," Alice said, coming back into the room again. "He's wanted to bring his sons home for such a long time. Perhaps he—"

"No harm? Of course, he meant no harm—no harm to himself! But what did he do to me? While he goes off to work in his fields, he expects me to perform miracles with his deaf son."

He shook his head. "I—didn't see it that way. Exactly."

"Well, that's the way it is. Exactly."

He reached for her hand. She drew it away. "Does this mean that—"

"That I'm walking out? Even before our marriage starts? I should! I'd have every right!" Juliette thought about the sweet face of the innocent, motherless boy she'd met only minutes before. His questioning eyes had broken her heart. He'd seemed so lost and in need of love. Her mind went to her baby. *If Andrew had been born deaf, I would never have turned my back on him.*

Alice remained silent.

Stone stood gaping, a look of defeat on his face. "I'll drive you back to the hotel, if you want."

She turned to the man with fire in her voice and tears in her eyes. "I'm so glad Will can't hear this conversation. He deserves so much more than this. I have no intention of running away and turning my back on him. That child needs love and a mother, and I intend to give him both."

Stone smiled gratefully, his eyes filling with tears. "I can't thank—"

"You're right!" she retorted sharply. "You can't thank me enough, because I don't want thanks. I want cooperation. Treat me like an adult, Stone. I may be young, but I am not a child and will not be treated as such." She rose, her hands on her hips. "And no more ordering me around. Do you hear me? I refuse to take orders. If you want me to do something, ask. If I decide to do it, I will. But don't order me to do it unless you want a rebellious woman on your hands. Now," she said, brushing her hands together and taking charge of the awkward situation. "Go get your boys and take them for a walk. Show them the horses or something. Just keep them busy while Alice and I have a woman-to-woman discussion."

"But I—"

"Stone."

"Yes, Juliette. Whatever you say."

Once he and the boys were out of the house, Juliette turned to her sister-in-law. "Now, I want to hear all about the boys—especially Will, and don't hold anything back. Tell me everything."

❧

At the first hint of dawn, Juliette climbed out of bed, careful not to waken her sleeping baby. She pulled her robe about her, then hurried down the hall to see if the woodstove needed another log added before Alice and the boys came down for breakfast. Only a few remaining embers penetrated the darkness, casting a dim glow. As she moved toward the stove, she tripped and nearly fell over something on the floor. It was something big and furry, and it was alive!

She let out a bloodcurdling scream and backed away in fear as she felt it move to stand beside her, its thick fur brushing against her leg.

Stone came running in, still in his nightshirt. "Help me!" she shouted as she grabbed for a nearby chair to defend herself.

He flung an arm about her waist and pulled her into his arms, lifting her flailing feet off the floor. She hugged his neck tightly, still screaming at the top of her lungs. "Get it out of here!"

"Kentucky, go," he said as he opened the door and let the would-be monster out into the cool morning air.

"Kentucky?" she repeated, still trembling with fear. "Who is Kentucky? *What* is Kentucky?"

Andrew wailed from his cradle. Eric tugged at his aunt's nightgown, his face buried in the folds.

"Everybody quiet down," Stone shouted above the maddening noise. "It's only Kentucky, my dog. He's perfectly harmless."

Juliette shoved him away from her. "A dog? You let him in the house?"

"Of course," Stone admitted with a grin that upset her even more. "He always sleeps in the house."

"Not anymore, he doesn't!" she stated flatly. "Not as long as I live here."

"But he's a good watchdog, and—"

"I don't care if he packs a gun, he is not sleeping in this house! Nor is he coming in here at any other time. Is that clear, Stone Piper?"

"Yes, Juliette. But a boy should have—"

"A boy should have a dog—outside! Not in the house. Dogs are smelly and unclean, and they shed. I refuse to have dog hair in my food. He's your dog. Keep him outside with you. I have no reason to get acquainted with him." With that she whipped around and went to take care of Andrew.

As she moved away, she heard Alice say, "You'd better listen to her, Stone. That woman is the right one for those boys. She's young, and she's got spunk and spirit. It's going to take all of that to mother these two boys—not to mention the patience it'll require to live with you. Be kind to her."

Juliette had difficulty getting back to sleep, knowing she'd behaved badly in front of her new family by causing such a scene. *I have to apologize,* she decided after much tossing and turning. *But there is no way I'm going to be able to live here with that big dog running in and out of this house.*

❧

For the next several weeks, Juliette added her own personal touches to their home while getting acquainted with Stone's boys. She saw very little of her husband. He spent most of his time outside, catching up on the tasks he'd neglected during his recovery. Some days, he donned his badge as Clacker County's deputy to fill in when the sheriff was absent.

Will was warming up a bit more each day. He loved playing with Andrew, and Andrew loved being around both Will and Eric. She found it easy to love Stone's boys. Their aunt Alice had done a good job raising them in their parents' absence. Andrew cooed to his new father each time he came into the house. He seemed to be accepting Stone's presence in his life.

Although Stone came in to have a quick lunch with them most every day, he rarely came into the house in the afternoon. Sometimes, rather than go into her room to nurse Andrew when the boys were upstairs taking their nap, Juliette would sit in Stone's chair in front of the fireplace, nursing her baby under the blanket, singing a lullaby to him as he suckled.

❧

Stone searched the house for Juliette. Finally noticing her door open, he realized she was probably in her room, putting Andrew down for a nap. He stepped into the room quietly. Then he stood transfixed.

The sight was too beautiful.

Lucy had never nursed their boys. She'd never wanted to. Although he'd wished she would have, he'd never pressed the issue.

He leaned slightly forward, wanting to get closer, to become a part of something so sweet and innocent. In his exuberance, he knocked a cup from the table, and it crashed to the floor, clanging loudly.

Juliette screamed and swept a shawl to cover herself.

Andrew, frightened by his mother's reaction and the crashing of the cup, began to howl.

Wide-eyed and consumed with guilt, Stone simply stared at her, not knowing what to say.

"You've been watching me!" Juliette yelled accusingly, clutching her baby tightly to her as she glared at him.

Eric came running down the stairs. Frightened and crying, he leapt into his father's arms.

"Now see what you've done?" she shrieked at him above her crying baby.

"I'm—I'm sorry. I didn't mean—"

"Whatever were you thinking?"

"I only wanted to—"

"To watch me? To spy on me? Have you forgotten our agreement?"

Stone hugged his son, then moved toward the door. "I won't let it happen again. Please forgive me. I would never—"

"Never?" She harrumphed. "You just did!"

He moved out the door without another word and quickly closed it behind him.

Soon things were back to normal. She and America worked on curtains for the boys' rooms, then prepared supper.

But Stone didn't come in at suppertime.

By bedtime, he still hadn't come into the house.

Juliette fed Andrew, tucked him in, pulled her cape about her shoulders, and lit a lamp. She was worried that something might have happened to her distraught husband.

She made her way to the barn and found him. He was in Blackie's stall, brushing the big horse. "Are you all right? I was concerned when you didn't come in for supper."

"I'm fine," he said quietly, keeping his back to her as he continued his brushing. "Don't fret about me."

"But I am concerned," she told him as she laid a hand on his shoulder. "Come on in. I'll warm up your supper. It's chilly out here in the barn."

"I—I figured I'd sleep out here tonight." He turned toward her. "I didn't think you'd want me in the house."

She stared at him. In the dim light of the lamp, she could detect an air of sadness on his wearied face. "This is *your* home, Stone. Of course I want you in the house."

"But—I broke my promise."

She moved a little closer to him. "You didn't do anything wrong. Not really."

"The minute I realized you were feeding Andrew, I should have gone back outside. But—but you were so beautiful, nursing your baby and singing to him. Once I'd entered the room and seen—"

"I should have shut my door. I realize that now. You scared me, that's all. I didn't know you'd come in the house. If I'd known, I would never have screamed like that."

"I should have coughed or something, I guess."

She touched his face with her fingertips. "You're forgiven. Now, come on in the house and have some supper."

She reached out her hand, and he took it. Holding the lamp ahead of them, she led him to the house.

№

The next evening, after Eric and Will had been tucked in for the night, Juliette took Andrew into her room to ready him for bed. Once she'd dressed him and settled herself in the small rocking chair, she covered herself with a blanket and began to feed her baby. She knew Stone was sitting in front of the fireplace. Normally, she would have shut the door, but this night she didn't.

Adjusting the blanket, she called out loudly enough for him to hear, "Stone, come in here, please."

He hurried to see what she wanted, but when he reached the door, he turned his head and drew back. "I've—I've done it again. I'm sorry. I'm really sorry."

She reached a hand out to him. "No, I called you. Come to me."

Surprised, he walked toward her, his gaze going everywhere

but to the blanket.

"I've thought a lot about yesterday," she began as she motioned for him to be seated in the chair across from her. "You *are* my husband, even though we've vowed not to share a marriage bed. There's no reason you shouldn't share in the joy I have in nursing my baby as long as I use a blanket. You can stay if you want to."

He leaned forward slightly. "Oh, Juliette, do you mean it? It's really all right if I stay?"

"Of course, I don't mind. Especially since you told me Lucy never nursed the boys. The two of you missed out on a wonderful experience. I love feeding my baby. It's a miracle from God that I not only gave him birth but can also give him the nourishment he needs."

Slowly, Stone leaned back in the chair and began to listen to the little noises coming from under the blanket as the baby nursed. "It is a miracle," he agreed in awe.

"You're always welcome in the room, Stone. Whenever I nurse my baby, we'll share the experience of this miracle together, as husband and wife."

A tear formed and trailed down his face. "Thank you, Juliette. You've made me very happy. I've missed out on so much, with my boys living in Missouri."

From beneath the blanket, Andrew gave a big sigh as he turned loose of his mother's breast.

"That's a beautiful sound," her husband said softly, turning his face away so Juliette had time to remove the blanket from the baby's face and adjust her clothing. "He's a lucky boy to have you as his mother."

"He is lucky. You've become the father he lost."

"I'll be a good father to him, Juliette. That's a promise."

❧

Long after Stone had gone to his room, Juliette lay in her bed, thinking. She had seen a softer, more caring side of this self-sufficient man—one she hadn't known existed. She liked what she'd seen.

She woke several hours later, stirred by a scraping noise she didn't recognize. *Has Stone let Kentucky in the house again?*

But as she listened, she became aware that the noise had a rhythm to it. No dog would make a sound like that, and it was coming from the other side of the wall. From the next room.

The locked room.

She crawled out of bed, pulled her door open quietly, and padded down the hall as the rhythmic sound continued. Careful not to make any noise, she felt the door's handle in search of the oversized padlock.

It was gone.

She stood there in the darkness, wondering who or what could be in that mysterious room. An intruder, maybe?

Should she awaken Stone?

Deciding that would be the logical thing to do, she moved down the hall to his room. To her surprise, his door stood wide open. In the moonlight that shone through his window, she could see his bed.

His empty bed.

It had to be Stone. But why? What could he be doing in there at this time of night?

She started to call out his name, but remembering how firm he'd been about her staying away from that room, decided against it. Perhaps he'd explain himself in the morning.

She padded back to bed and tried to get back to sleep, but the constant sound seemed to magnify in the darkness.

Eventually, the sound ceased. She heard the door open and close, the sound of the padlock being put back in place, then her husband's bedroom door being closed.

Why was her husband so adamant about keeping her out of there? What could possibly be of that much importance to him? And why did he go in there long after he thought the rest of the household had bedded down for the night?

Of one thing she was certain. That room held more than storage items. *Someday,* she told herself, *even though I know I told him I'd stay out of there, Stone is going to forget to lock that door. And if he does, I just might have myself a quick peek. After all, what could it hurt? I am his wife now. There shouldn't be any secrets between us, should there?*

❧

Stone being in the room while Juliette nursed Andrew soon became a nightly ritual in the Piper household. It was a precious time for both of them, a time for them to be together, alone, to share in conversation and wonderment. It also had become a ritual for Stone to lean over and kiss the sleeping baby after Juliette placed him in the crib, just before saying good night to her.

For her birthday, Stone gave her a beautiful gelding she named Diamond because of the unusual marking across his nose. She and Stone spent many pleasant hours together, riding through the pasture and down by the river. She enjoyed their many conversations and the way Stone treated her like an intelligent woman as they discussed his ranching business.

Through her tutelage, Eric could now read the simplest of words. She'd been working with Will too, and he had become her shadow. Things were going well in the Piper household.

One afternoon during a hard rain, at his wife's insistence, Stone decided to take a few hours off and spend them with his family.

"Stone, look into Will's eyes and, very slowly, with an exaggerated movement of your mouth, say, 'I love you.' "

Stone frowned. "Why?"

"Go head. Do it."

He pulled the boy onto his lap. "I—love—you."

A gigantic smile broke across the child's face. Then, in his strange, high-pitched voice, he answered, "Ah—wuv—ooh, da da."

Stone began to weep openly. "It's a miracle!" he shouted as he leapt to his feet and began whirling his son about the room. "You can talk. You can actually talk!"

"It's a beginning," Juliette said with pride. "We're working on it every day. Soon, there'll be more."

Tears flowed down his cheeks unashamedly. "I'm sorry to admit it, but at times, Will didn't seem like a real person to me. He was off in his own dream world, and I couldn't penetrate it. But you've gotten through to him. How did you do it, Juliette? What's your secret?"

She beamed as he lowered his son to the floor and sat down beside her. "Love. It's that simple, Stone. That boy needed the love of people who cared for him. Between the two of us, we're giving it to him."

Stone slipped an arm about her waist, pulled her close to him, and pressed her head against his chest. "Having you here has changed our lives, Juliette. How can I ever repay you?"

"Seeing my husband and our boys happy and secure is all the payment I'll ever need. Being your wife has changed my life too." She offered a slight chuckle. "Oh, I'll admit I had doubts our arrangement would work, but I'm quite happy living here on Carson Creek Ranch and being Mrs. Stone Piper. You're a fine husband."

He tightened his grip and kissed the top of her head before nestling his face in her hair. "I'm glad you're my wife."

૨ð

"Today is a very special day."

Juliette stopped sweeping and leaned the broom against the wall. "Someone's birthday?"

Stone shook his head. "Nope. Not a birthday."

She brushed aside a lock of hair and frowned. "What, then?"

"Woman, it's our third-month anniversary! Did you forget?"

"Three months? How can that be? How the time has flown!"

"Well," he began, taking her hand in his and drawing her close, "I didn't forget. I've planned something special."

Before she could respond, the door opened, and her sister burst in. "Are the boys ready to go? Father is waiting in the buggy."

Juliette's brows lifted, and her eyes widened. "The boys

ready? What're you talking about, Caroline? What's going on here?"

"She's here to take the boys into town for the afternoon so we can go on a picnic together down by the river. Just the two of us. America is already preparing our basket."

"Come on, boys," Caroline instructed Eric and Will as she wrapped Andrew in his blanket. "Grandfather is waiting for us." She grabbed the bag America had prepared and headed out the door. She called over her shoulder, "We'll bring them back in a couple of hours. Have fun!"

Minutes later, as the couple walked across the meadow holding hands, laughing, and talking like old married folks, Kentucky ran up behind them and began jumping onto his master's legs.

"Does Kentucky have to come?" Juliette came to a halt, her arms crossed over her chest.

"He won't bother us, he's—"

"Stone, please! You know how I feel about dogs."

"Go, Kentucky," he told the excited dog as the friendly animal circled around him, barking and nipping at his heels. "Go home."

She stood on tiptoe and kissed his cheek. "I'm truly happy. Aren't you?"

"You know I am." He wrapped his arms about her and gazed into her eyes. "Are you ever sorry you married me?"

She braced her hands against his chest and looked up at him, her expression becoming solemn. "Of course I'm not sorry. I love being married to you. I love your children. But I have to admit—sometimes, when I'm all alone in that empty bed at night, I miss the closeness I had with David. There's nothing as comforting as cuddling up in bed next to the man you love."

Quickly donning a smile, she pushed away and ran in the direction of the river. "But I knew that would never happen again when I decided to become Mrs. Stone Piper. I've resolved not to let it bother me."

He hurried to catch up with her, the picnic basket swinging

in his hand. By the time he caught her, she'd already reached the river and was sitting on the tattered quilt America sent along. He sat down beside her and watched as she began to pull things from the basket.

"I'm—I'm sorry, Juliette," he told her, hanging his head. "I know I can never take David's place. You're young and so beautiful. You could've had your pick of men. Handsome, witty men. Single men, without the burden of children to care for. I should never have forced you into this arrangement."

"Forced? You think I was forced into it?" she quipped with a mischievous laugh as she pulled the last of the food from the basket. "No one forces me into anything. You, of all people, should know how stubborn I am. You could never have put this ring on my finger, Stone Piper, if I hadn't been in agreement."

"But—"

"Look, it's our anniversary. Let's forget such foolishness and have some fun. This is our day, and I aim to enjoy it." She touched her finger to the tip of his nose with a giggle. "Don't be such an old worrier."

He took her hand in his as he gave her a broad smile. "You win! But remember this, Juliette: If being married to me ever becomes too much for you, I'll let you go."

"You'll never get rid of me, Stone. I'm here to stay." She broke from his grasp, leapt to her feet, and ran along the river's edge. Twisting and motioning for him to follow, she teased, "Bet you can't catch me!"

Stone rose quickly and took off after her. When he caught her, he held her tight as she struggled to free herself.

When all her energy had been spent, she relaxed in his arms. Then, she leaned into him and looked up into his eyes. It took all her resolve to keep from kissing him and telling him how important he had become to her. Just the touch of his hand made her giddy. Was this love?

"I'm hungry," he finally said, releasing her from his grasp. "How about you?"

Straightening her frock, she headed toward the quilt they'd

left spread on the ground. "Me too."

But even as they enjoyed their food, Juliette couldn't get her mind off Kentucky and the look of disappointment on Stone's face when he'd sent the dog away. *As usual, I've been unreasonable, putting my own needs above those of my husband's. It wouldn't have hurt one bit if that dog had come along with us.*

Lord, forgive me and, please, make me more like You.

⋆

The next afternoon, after Stone had gone back to the barn and the older boys were taking their nap, Juliette carried Andrew to a grassy spot outside and let him lie on a blanket while she went back into the house to get her basket of laundry. By the time she'd hung the wash on the line, he was fast asleep. *I'll just leave him here while I go grab a few more things to wash. He should be fine. I'll only be gone a few minutes.*

With one final glance toward her child, she carried her empty basket into the house and gathered a few of the baby's small garments.

Suddenly, Kentucky began barking loudly. "That dog! He must be near Andrew!" she said with disgust, as she dropped a tiny gown, grabbed the broom from behind the door, and ran outside.

She was right. The big dog was near Andrew. And he was snarling and baring his teeth. But not at the baby. At a wolf!

Juliette knew she could never run the vicious wolf off with a broom. Hoping Kentucky would be able to hold him at bay, she ran back into the house and pulled Stone's revolver from its hiding place. When she reached the porch, she lifted the gun into the air and fired.

Boom!

The wolf took off across the field.

She fired a second shot. *Boom!*

Quickly, she placed the gun on the railing and rushed toward her screaming baby, who had already begun to crawl off the pallet. After grabbing Andrew, she ran into the house and slammed the door behind her. Her mind raced with thoughts of what might have happened if Kentucky hadn't been there.

Eric was standing in the middle of the room crying, wakened from a sound sleep. She looked around for Will, then realized his sleep probably hadn't been interrupted. He may not even have heard the shots.

With her baby in her arms, she took Eric's hand, led him to the rocking chair, and tried to calm them both.

The door burst open, and Stone came running in with Kentucky in his arms. The dog wasn't moving. "What happened? I heard the gunshot and came running. I found Kentucky—"

Juliette gasped. The dog was bleeding profusely, his blood flowing over his master. "Is—is he—dead?"

"No, he's still alive, but he's very weak. He's lost a lot of blood." Stone knelt and lowered Kentucky onto the small rug in front of the fireplace. "Why did you shoot him, Juliette? He's done nothing to you," he asked sadly as he stroked the dog's back.

"Me, shoot him? I didn't shoot him! He saved Andrew's life! I fired at the wolf!" she screamed in defense of her actions. "If it weren't for him, Andrew might have been killed!"

"I–I didn't know." Stone dipped a rag in the pail of water heating on the woodstove and began to wipe at the dog's wounds. "He's alive—but barely."

Juliette placed Andrew on the pallet and fell to her knees beside him. She began to cry as she stared at the blood-soaked fur. "He has to live. Oh, Stone, make Kentucky live. Please."

"I don't know. That wolf really did a job on him. Juliette." He paused and swallowed hard. "He's missing an eye."

"An eye?" She crumpled into a ball on the floor, her face cupped in her hands. "It's all my fault. If I hadn't left Andrew in the yard. If only I'd—"

His arm wrapped tightly about her. "You did the right thing."

Her tears flowed profusely. "That brave dog! If only I hadn't been so cruel to him. If I'd—"

He stood and pulled her up with him. "I've got to get him to Doc Meeker. He'll know what to do. Stay here with the boys. I'll be back as soon as I can."

"But I want to help—"

"Then pray. Be prepared—Kentucky might not make it. From the looks of things, his wounds are pretty deep, and with that eye gone—well, we'll just have to wait and see."

Juliette placed Andrew's blanket over the bleeding dog. "Wrap him in this, Stone. He'll need to be kept warm."

Carefully, he wrapped the blanket about the animal's limp body. "But this is Andrew's blanket."

Her tear-filled eyes met his. "Without Kentucky, there might not be an Andrew."

*

Stone returned four long hours later with Kentucky wrapped in the blood-soaked blanket. "Doc did everything for him he could. All we can do now is take care of him, pray, and hope he makes it."

The two took turns keeping vigil over the injured dog for three days and nights. Praying over him. Urging him to drink and eat. Encouraging him to get better. On the fourth day, during Juliette's watch, Kentucky lifted his head.

She hollered for Stone, then bent and kissed the dog between his drooping ears. "Oh, Kentucky, Kentucky. You're a hero too."

"This dog a hero?" Stone teased as he hurried to her side. "Is this the same dog who was banished from the house? The dog who wasn't allowed to go on picnics with us?"

She leaned into her husband and rested her head on his shoulder. "If only I'd known what a fine dog he is. The only dog I ever got close to was our neighbor's dog in Ohio. He bit my hand when I was three." She held up her hand and showed him a nearly invisible, jagged scar. "I've never forgotten. I've always been terribly afraid of dogs."

"I guess you know now, Kentucky would never hurt anyone."

She stroked the dog's back lovingly. "Yes, I know. And, Kentucky," she said pulling her hair away from her face and leaning close to the dog's ear. "This is your home too. Come in anytime you want. You can even sleep in my room."

Stone reared back with a loud burst of laughter. "Now I'd say that's quite a concession. What can *I* do to get into your good graces like Kentucky?"

She smiled up at him. "You already are."

"Well, I'd say your loving care is what's going to put that dog back on his feet, if anything will."

"Is he really going to be all right?"

As if on cue, Kentucky tried to stand. Stone lowered him back onto the rug. "Looks like it to me."

❧

Within weeks, Kentucky was running about the yard during the day and spending his nights curled up at the foot of Juliette's bed. Still not used to maneuvering around with only one eye, he would bump into things occasionally. Although the sight tore at the hearts of the adults, the boys would laugh at his awkwardness.

❧

"I have to make a trip to Topeka tomorrow," Stone an-nounced one afternoon several weeks later, "to take a look at some cattle one of their local men will be selling. Will you and the children be all right while I'm gone?"

"We'll be fine," she assured him. "Don't worry about us."

He crossed the room and pulled his valise from a shelf. "I'll leave first thing in the morning, but don't get up."

Stone pulled Juliette into his arms and planted a kiss on her forehead. "I'll be back in a few days. If you need anything, send Moses into town."

She waited until he was asleep, then lit her lamp and wrote him a note. Quietly, after rubbing one of the sweet-smelling bars of soap across the page, she slipped it into his valise.

nine

He frowned, picked up the little paper, and carefully unfolded it, noting a sweet, sweet fragrance that reminded him of the wife he'd left behind in Dove City.

> *Dearest Stone,*
>   *I wanted to tell you how much I enjoy being your wife and a mother to Eric and Will. But I find it's hard to put it into words. If I had my pick of husbands, I'd choose you. I feel privileged to bear the name, Mrs. Stone Piper. I'll miss you. Hurry home to us.*
>
>   *All my love,*
>   *Juliette.*

Stone rubbed at his tired eyes and reread her note. Especially the signature line. Smiling, he sat down on the side of the bed, tugged off a boot, and wiggled his toes. *Hmm, all my love, huh?*

The smile quickly changed to a frown as the second boot hit the floor with a *kerplunk. Most likely she's just happy to have a nice place for her and her son to live.* This time, he lifted the paper to his nose and breathed in the pleasant aroma. *I've sure got me a fine woman. Beautiful too.*

After refolding the note and slipping it back into his valise, he climbed into bed, crossed his arms behind his head, and lay staring at the ceiling. *I promised her I'd leave her alone, and I meant it. I aim to keep my promise.*

With a grunt, he flipped over onto his side and tugged the covers over his head. *Sometimes, I want to grab that woman and kiss her like she's never been kissed.*

Eventually he drifted off to sleep with dreams of a lovely

young woman standing on her tiptoes, planting a good-bye kiss on his lips.

&

Since it was still much too early to begin preparing breakfast, Juliette decided to wash out the shirt Stone had worn the day before he left. As usual, she found his room immaculate. She pulled the shirt from its peg, knowing he'd be pleased to find it freshly laundered when he returned. She was about to dunk it into the wash water when she felt something hard in the pocket. A key. A large key. Like one that would fit a padlock.

Her heart raced. Could it be a key for one of the boarded-up areas in the barn? Maybe it was the key to the padlock on the mysterious room.

Remembering Stone's admonition, she slipped it into her apron pocket, fully planning to place it on the floor, just under the edge of his bed, after she'd finished washing his shirt. He'd think it had fallen out of his pocket when he'd hung it on the peg and never suspect she'd found it.

Perhaps it is the key to a padlock out in the barn and not the key to the mysterious room, after all, she kept telling herself. The key seemed to grow heavier and heavier in her pocket with each passing moment.

If the key *was* the key for the padlock on the mysterious room, what would one tiny peek hurt? Stone would never even have to know. *He told me to stay out of that room!* her heart said. But the little voice inside her head answered back, *Go ahead. Look. He is your husband. There shouldn't be any secrets between the two of you. As his wife, you have every right to know what's in that room.*

She stood gazing at the key. *Why? Why would Stone want to keep me out of there? It doesn't make any sense.*

Slipping the key back into her pocket, she hurried outside to hang his shirt on the line. The longer the key remained in her pocket, the more curious she became. It nagged at her, goading her to try it in the padlock.

Finally, once the boys were down for their afternoon nap,

she crept down the hall to the locked room.

With trembling hands, she lifted the heavy padlock and inserted the key. "Forgive me, Stone," she whimpered softly, "but I have to try it."

She counted to three, giving herself time to change her mind. Knowing, if the key fit and she used it, she'd not only be invading her husband's privacy but disobeying his orders.

She gave it a turn.

The padlock opened.

Still trembling, and feeling like an intruder, she removed the lock and warily pushed open the door, intending to take a quick peek, then close and lock it. Her mind was filled with all sorts of things she thought she might find in there. Tools. Packing crates. Old clothes. Musty-smelling books. Cobwebs. Spiders.

But none of those things were what greeted her as she hesitantly pushed open the door.

Instead, she found a room with sunlight flowing in through expensive, imported lace curtains. The room was filled with French furniture—an ornate chest of drawers, a carved bed head, and an upholstered rocker. Her breath caught in her throat. *The rocker. Of course! That's the rhythmic creaking sound I've been hearing during the night. Stone has been rocking in that rocker. But why?*

She stood in the doorway, trying to convince herself to walk away, but she couldn't. Tiptoeing carefully, knowing she shouldn't be touching anything but unable to resist, she opened drawers, peeked in boxes, sorted through stacks of linens, and quickly scanned each area of the lovely room. Although she found many items she would like to have for herself, she left everything in its place. It had to have been Lucy's room!

She held a lovely silk-fringed scarf to her cheek, reveling in its softness. Had Stone kept all these things locked away, thinking she would be jealous of his dead wife if she saw them? That she would be unable to live with Lucy's things around her as a constant reminder of the woman he'd said he'd loved more than life itself?

After folding the scarf and putting it carefully back into its place, she lifted a heavily embellished lace camisole and held it to her bosom. *What a lady Lucy must have been. No wonder Stone has never been able to get her out of his mind.* She caught sight of her reflection in the tiny mirror hanging above a delicately carved dressing table. *Each time Stone looks at me he must be thinking about Lucy! Is that why, at times, he seems moody and distant?*

Being careful to refold the camisole into its original shape, she placed it alongside the scarf, still awed by its beauty. She'd never owned lovely silky things like Lucy's. A tear rolled down her cheek as she remembered the pristine white hanky Stone had given her. She couldn't help smiling at the dear, awkward way he'd presented it to her.

Deciding she'd seen more than enough, she started for the door. But on her way, she caught sight of a beautiful carved chest, quite large by most standards, which stood in the far corner.

She paused long enough to lift the lid, carefully working her way through its contents. Each piece she found in the chest was even lovelier than the piece before it. *What fine things Lucy had*, she marveled as she fingered a delicate, beaded, silk purse, trying to imagine where the woman would carry such a costly thing. It seemed Stone's first wife had had nothing but the finest of everything.

Next, she found a large, silk drawstring bag containing at least a dozen beautiful handmade Christmas ornaments, many with beads and bangles sewn onto them. She wondered about the Christmas trees Lucy must have decorated with Stone's help. *How sad she died so young, when she had so much for which to live.*

She lifted several layers of intricately embroidered pillowcases and table scarves, but something on the bottom caught her attention. There, neatly stacked together and tied with a red silk ribbon, she found twelve beautifully hand-pieced Flower Basket quilt blocks. In the corner of each one, some-one had embroidered the name, Lucy Piper. Probably Lucy herself. *She must have died before she finished this magnificent quilt,* Juliette thought sadly as she examined each block and its perfect, tiny stitches.

She placed the blocks back into their corner of the chest, alongside the folds of fabric already cut for the backing and the sashing of the quilt. But as her fingers touched the wonderful blocks, an idea occurred to her. *I'll finish the quilt for Stone for Christmas! That'll show my husband I'm not offended by having Lucy's things around me.*

She glanced around, taking in the many crystal vases, fancy pillows, framed pictures, and such. *Stone's boys deserve to see the things their mother held dear. Wouldn't it be nice if, because of my finishing the quilt for Stone and letting him know I don't mind having Lucy's things around, he would open this room and allow the children to see and enjoy their mother's belongings?*

She removed the fabric and the blocks, holding them close to her as she began to dance about the room. *What a delicious idea. He'll be so pleased. I can just imagine the look on his face on Christmas Day when I present him with Lucy's quilt.*

She hurriedly put the rest of the things back into the chest, closing the lid with a satisfied smile. *This is going to be so much fun. My stitches may not be as perfect as Lucy's, but I'm sure Stone will never notice. He'll be so happy to see the finished quilt.*

She hurried into her room, slipped her treasure into a box beneath her bed, then rushed to close the door and secure it with the padlock before placing the key on the floor in his room.

❧

Three days later, Stone walked into his house, hoping he'd be met with the same kind of kiss as his good-bye kiss. But all he got from his wife was a smile and a look that told him she had something on her mind she wasn't about to share with him.

જી

With discontent among the local Indians and many land disputes, Stone, Zach Nance, and the others found themselves spending much of their time keeping peace between the Indians and the landowners. Juliette hated his being gone so much of the time. While she couldn't understand why he felt responsible to ride with the men every time the sheriff was out of town or something happened, it did give her time to work on the quilt.

And although Stone kept close-mouthed about much of what he did, her father kept her well informed of her husband's heroism, bravery, and talents as a tactful negotiator.

જી

Two days before Christmas, Stone brought home a tree he'd cut from their pasture. The smell of freshly cut pine filled the house as Juliette and the children made crude ornaments from popcorn, paper, twigs, and string. All the time they were making them, she thought about the lovely ornaments in the trunk in Lucy's room, wondering why Stone didn't get them for their tree.

She and America set about making gingerbread cookies, poking holes in some of them, and threading ribbons through the holes so the miniature gingerbread men could be hung on the tree. Even little Will kept repeating in his strange, high-pitched voice, "Twee. Twee. Twee."

Stone would laugh loudly as his son repeated the word over and over, then he'd pull Will onto his lap and place the child's hands on his throat. "Christmas. Say, Christmas."

With a smile that touched his father's heart, Will responded. "Kwis—mass. Aa Kwis-mass."

Stone's eyes filled with tears as he hugged the boy. "Hearing you speak is the most wonderful Christmas present a father could have. Oh, Juliette, you've done wonders with my son. I'm so grateful."

Once the boys were settled down for the night and the house turned quiet, the couple sat on the floor in front of the tree. Stone leaned against a chair and pulled Juliette close to him. "We have quite a family, don't we?"

She nodded and snuggled back into his arms contentedly.

"So, if you could have your pick of husbands, you would pick me?"

She sighed and pulled his arms closer about her. "Uh huh."

"You still mean it?"

"I wrote it, didn't I?"

"Sometimes folks say what they think other folks want to hear."

"Is that what you think I did?"

"I hope not. I'd like to think you meant it."

"I did."

The next two days were busy as Juliette put the last few stitches in the quilt by lamplight, long after Stone had gone to bed. When it came time for them to open their gifts, the quilt had been finished, folded, and placed in a lovely box her mother had given her, ready to be presented to her husband.

⛬

"Christmas is a special time," Stone began Christmas morning as he pulled out his big Bible and gathered his precious family around him. "It's when we celebrate the birth of the baby Jesus." He opened it to the second chapter of Luke and read the Christmas story. He prayed and asked God to bless each one present and draw each member of their little family close to Him and to one another.

The children unwrapped their gifts, then spent most of the day playing with the few toys Stone had either made for them or purchased in Topeka. Later that evening, Juliette clapped her hands to get their sons' attention. "Time for cider and cookies, then off to bed. You boys have had quite a busy day."

"I have a present for you," Stone said with a grin, once the children had been tucked in for the night.

She smiled demurely. "A Christmas present for me?"

He took her hand and led her to his room. Her heart pounded. Was he going to ask her to share his bed? Lately he'd certainly shown signs of caring deeply for her. She wondered how she should respond if he did. Should she seem surprised? Resist his advances? Remind him again of their vows? Or fall into his arms and hope he showered her with kisses? After all, they *were* married. It would be perfectly proper for them to share his bed.

"Close your eyes," he told her as they were about to enter his room. "Open them."

There, in the middle of the room, stood a beautiful hand-carved chest much like the one she'd seen in Lucy's room with flowers, birds, and trees adorning it.

"I made it for you. I hope you like it."

She bent low and ran her fingers over the delicate carving, overcome by his magnificent gift. "But when did you do this?"

"I worked nights, after you'd gone to bed. Other times I'd get up in the early morning darkness and go to the barn to work on it. I wanted to make something special for you, something with my own hands."

"Oh, Stone. I love it. Thank you." She crossed the room and threw her arms about his neck.

His lips met hers and, for the first time, she felt the ghost of Lucy was no longer standing between them as his kisses trailed down her neck. It was as if suddenly his pent-up emotions had been released. As quickly as he'd pulled her to him, he pushed her away. "I'm sorry. I should never have done that."

Disappointed but excited about the gift she had for him, she grabbed his hand and tugged him back to the living room. "Sit here. I'll be right back."

She hurried into her room and pulled the box from beneath her bed, then rushed back to him, her heart pounding with anticipation. "Here, this is for you."

"Aw, you didn't have to get me a present."

"Open it." She seated herself beside him and waited expectantly.

He untied the ribbon, removed the lid, and lifted the quilt

from the box. But the appreciation and joy she'd expected to find on his face were not there. Instead, his face twisted with anger and took on a look of shock.

"You've been in Lucy's room!" The sound of his infuriated voice echoed through the house.

He shouted at her with such wrath, it frightened her, and she pulled away from him. Her heart was broken by his outrageous response, and she feared he'd wake the children.

"What right did you have to go in there after I told you to stay out!"

"I only—"

"I had a padlock on that door! That room belonged to Lucy!" He moved about the room, knocking chairs over, brushing things off tables, kicking at anything in sight. "I forbade you to go in that room, and you disobeyed me!"

She stood and faced him squarely, needing him to understand her motives. "I'm your wife now! Me! Juliette! Not Lucy! Must everything be a shrine to her?"

"You're only a substitute." He clutched the quilt in his arms, grabbed his jacket from the hook, and rushed out the door, slamming it behind him.

Juliette stared at the door. What had she done that had been so awful? She'd only wanted to make him happy.

She waited up for him until after midnight, then went into her room to think. She could no longer live with this man. He'd offered to let her go. Perhaps she should accept his offer. *But what'll become of Will? And Eric? Will they have to go back to St. Joseph? And what about Andrew and me? Will I be able to find work that pays enough to support the two of us?*

She crawled into her bed and wept most of the night, crying out to God for wisdom. She loved this man.

⋆

Stone didn't come back in the house until noon the next day. He'd spent the night in the barn, warring with himself about the gamut of emotions he'd been experiencing since Juliette had come into his life. On one hand, he'd been sulking about her blatant disregard for his orders. On the other, he'd battled with the overwhelming desire to rush back into the house, take her in his arms, apologize, and make her truly, completely his—despite what he'd promised her.

"I'm glad you're back. We have to talk," Juliette told him after they'd finished their lunch. "Tonight, after the chores are done."

He nodded, keeping his face expressionless. "Fine."

As he made his way back to the barn, Zach Nance rode into the yard and hurriedly dismounted. "Stone," he said, trying to catch his breath. "The brothers of the man who died at the MacGregor place have been in town, bragging they're gonna kill you to avenge their brother's death. They also said their gang is gonna rob some of the banks in the area."

"Got any idea which banks?"

The man nodded. "I'm afraid so. A rider came into town just before I left. He said they've already hit the Gordon City bank this morning. He overheard one of the men say the Bartonville bank was gonna be next."

"Let me get my guns." Stone ran to the barn, gathered up what he'd need, and returned riding Blackie. "Let's go."

"Aren't you going to tell Juliette you're leaving?"

Stone shook his head. "She'll find out soon enough, not that she cares. Let's go. Maybe we can intercept them before they get to Bartonville."

❧

Juliette watched from the window. What had Zach Nance said to Stone? Why had they ridden off so fast? Well, if he'd wanted her to know, he would have told her. Obviously, he no longer thought of her as an important part of his life.

She told America to take the rest of the day off and went about tidying up the house. She took down the Christmas tree and the few decorations she'd placed throughout their home.

Several times during the long night, Juliette tiptoed down the hall to see if her husband had slipped in undetected. The empty bed confirmed her suspicions. If only she'd heard his conversation with Mr. Nance, she might have had a clue as to his whereabouts.

By noon the next day, worry had replaced her concern. She spent the afternoon packing up the things that belonged to her and Andrew and placing them in the buggy in preparation for moving back to the hotel. She'd just carried the last box to the buggy when a man she'd seen her husband speaking with in town several weeks earlier came riding into the yard looking for Stone.

"I'm sorry, my husband isn't here. I'm not sure when he'll be back," she told the man, embarrassed at her lack of knowledge.

"Actually, I've come to warn Deputy Piper," the out-of-breath man said hurriedly. "In the saloon last night, I overheard one of the Dighton boys saying they were going to find Stone and kill him to avenge their brother's death. I'm sure they meant it. The deputy needs to know so he can be on his guard. Those men mean business. Tell him to be careful!"

Juliette thanked him, then watched as he rode out of the yard. *I've got to let Stone know!*

Forgetting all about leaving for the hotel, she raced to the barn, screaming at Moses to help her saddle up Diamond. After grabbing a shawl, one of Stone's heaviest jackets, and a woolen scarf from a hook by the door, she shouted out orders to Moses, telling him to have America stay with the children until she returned and to keep their guns handy. She waved, then rode out in search of her husband.

⁂

Stone and his band of volunteers spent the rest of the day searching the area near Gordon City. The entire night, they hovered in the graveyard next to the bank in Bartonville. If the band of outlaws hit the place, as they'd said they were going to, he and his men would be ready for them.

The bank opened at ten as usual. Other than the few regular customers who showed up, there didn't seem to be much activity.

"Think they've outfoxed us?" Stone finally asked Zach

Nance several hours later. "Maybe they started that rumor to throw us off the trail. You think they might have lured us out of town so they could hit our bank in Dove City?"

"Don't know." Mr. Nance stretched first one arm, then the other as he arched his back. "There sure isn't anything going on around here. I think we'd better head for home. That way, if we are needed, we'll be a whole lot closer than we are now."

Stone signaled the group of men, and they rode back toward town. When they reached the cutoff to Carson Creek Ranch, he saluted and headed Blackie toward home. "Let me know if you need me, and I'll come running."

But as he turned Blackie into the yard, Moses came rushing out of the house, his arms flailing about wildly. "Juliette's gone!"

Stone let out a sorrowful sigh. *So she couldn't even wait for us to have our talk. She's already left me.*

"She rode off on Diamond lookin' for you!" Moses cried out. "The Dighton brothers said they was gonna kill you!"

Stone's heart sank. He reined up and leaped off Blackie. "Where are the children?"

Moses bent to catch his breath. "With America."

Stone pounded his palm against his forehead. "I should never have left her like I did!" Reminding Moses to keep himself armed, he rode out on Blackie in search of his wife.

❧

Juliette maneuvered Diamond through the trees along the river's edge, snagging her clothing, catching her long hair on the branches and brambles until exhaustion overtook her and she could go no farther. Why hadn't she found Stone? Perhaps he hadn't even come this way. Perhaps she'd been going in circles. Disgusted by her lack of tracking skills and growing more concerned over her husband, she began to cry. *Why did I come out here all alone? Did I actually think I could find Stone?*

The sudden hoot of an owl sent shivers down her back.

Lord God, she pled as her tears flowed freely. *Protect me, please. You know how afraid I am. Most of all, protect my husband. His children need him.* She wiped at her tears. *I—I need him. I love him so much. I have to tell him.*

Thinking she heard voices off in the distance, she paused to listen. The voices weren't those of Stone and his men, but the voices of the band of outlaws! Maybe they had a lookout. Maybe two or three, and she'd be discovered! Terrified, she scrambled off Diamond and cautiously led him through the dense trees. She tried to be quiet, yet put as much distance as possible between her and her potential captors without attracting their attention. *Those men would like nothing better than to find Deputy Stone Piper's wife alone in the woods and at their mercy.* She trembled at the thought.

Mounting Diamond again when she reached an open area, she rode for what seemed like hours until the late afternoon turned into evening. She constantly listened for sounds of riders, keeping an eye on the sky and the rapidly approaching storm. She was hopelessly lost and had no idea which direction she should go to reach the ranch.

Suddenly, a bolt of lightning split the sky and thunder rumbled overhead, spooking Diamond. The horse reared, throwing her to the ground before taking off through the trees and disappearing into the darkness.

Excruciating pain consumed her body. Sure her arm had been broken in her fall, Juliette lay crying on the ground, her head bleeding from where she'd hit it on a rock. "Oh, Stone, Stone, where are you?" she whispered as she cradled her aching arm close to her body. She was afraid if she called out, the outlaws might hear her. "I need you!"

The rain began to fall, as thunder growled fiercely and lightning flashed across the night sky. *I have to find shelter*, she told herself as she struggled to her feet. After much searching, she discovered a huge, fallen tree with a rotting cavern in its side just big enough to hold her. Feeling woozy from the bump on her head and clutching her arm tightly to her, she bent low and worked her body into the elongated opening. "I–I'm so co–cold. I'm not sure I can ma–make it through the ni–night," she mumbled through chattering teeth, working to pull Stone's wet jacket close about her to ward off the brisk night air. *Stone will never find me here, but I can't stay out in the storm all night.*

After pulling a few leaves and brush about her to fend off the cold, Juliette closed her eyes and tried to sleep. But sleep wouldn't come. *I was stupid to have ridden out here by myself! It was a crazy thing to do. I should've gone into town and tried to find Thomas Ward. But I had to come! I was so worried about Stone. What if that man found him?*

Suddenly, she felt something touch her side—something furry. She froze with fear, remembering the look on the wolf's face as he'd bared his teeth in her yard that day. *Oh God,* she prayed, holding her breath and trying hard not to move. *Have I escaped those men only to be eaten alive by some wild animal? What will become of my baby without me there to care for him? Help me!*

A single flash of lightning made her worst fears a reality. An animal of some kind was creeping low across the ground, circling her, and she knew her life was about to come to an end. She closed her eyes and held her breath. *Oh, God, please don't let me die! Not now! Not yet! Not this way!*

Instead of attacking her, the animal began licking her face! Her heart pounded furiously, and she tried to back away, but the stump prevented it. As another flash of lightning split the sky, she caught sight of the gentle, one-eyed face of Kentucky.

"Oh, Kentucky, you dear, sweet dog," she told him as she wrapped her good arm about him. "You followed me!"

Kentucky licked at her wounds, then settled down beside her, sharing the warmth of his body. She praised God for answering her prayer and sending the big dog to comfort her and keep her warm.

"You're almost as good as an angel."

❧

"Not much use looking for her in this darkness. Let's go.

Maybe Juliette's already back home waiting for us." Faint with feelings of discouragement and defeat, Stone turned Blackie around and headed for the ranch.

"Sorry, Stone, I ain't seen Juliette," Moses told him as he rode into the yard. "She never came home."

Shaking the rain off his hat, Stone turned and rode out of the yard again. "She'll freeze out there. I've got to find her!"

Hours later, he dismounted Blackie, tied his reins to a sapling, and fell on the ground, striking it with his fists. "God," he called out, confident the God of heaven would hear his cries. "I've sinned against You something awful, and I've sinned against others. There's been so much unrighteousness in my life. More'n most folks would believe."

He swallowed at the lump in his throat as tears of repentance flowed down his cheeks. "Only You know what a fake I've been—pretending to be this fine, upstanding Christian man, when deep inside, I was nothing but a lying scoundrel. The Bible says You are faithful and just to forgive our sins. I'm begging You to forgive mine. I'm accepting Christ as my Savior. Cleanse me, Lord. Come into my heart. Come into my life. Take over, God. I'm Yours now. My life is in Your hands now."

As he lay in the rain, communing with God, a sweet peace came over him. He knew God had heard and answered his plea. With a newfound faith, he began to pray again.

"God, I've done wrong to the finest woman I've ever known. Don't let her suffer because of me. She's got a little boy who needs her." He paused and lifted his eyes heavenward. The rain fell upon his face and his shoulders, soaking his jacket. "I need her. I–I—love her. Watch over her, please. Bring her back to me. Give me another chance to do right by her. I promise I'll tell her everything."

He stood and listened to the night, hoping for a sound that would lead him to his wife. But the only sounds he heard were those of the whining of the wind as it whipped through the trees and the thunder rolling about overhead.

The storm finally over, the sky began to lighten somewhat

as Stone sat crouched beside Blackie. He'd searched the entire night. *Juliette, sweet, sweet Juliette, where are you? If only I would've told you how much I love you!*

He stared at the sky as streaks of red, pink, and blue lifted themselves above the horizon. *She always loved the sunrise,* he reminded himself as the splendor of the new day dawned before him.

Wearily, he rose and mounted his horse. "Which way now, Blackie?" he asked, stroking the horse's mane. As he turned to take one last look at the sunrise, something caught his eye. Something moved by a huge fallen log several yards ahead of him. It looked like a wolf or a coyote. He couldn't be sure.

Curious, he slowly edged Blackie closer. It *was* an animal of some sort, all right, and it almost looked like his big dog. He blinked and looked again. It *was* his big dog! *But why would Kentucky be out here in the woods? Did he follow me?*

He called to him, but the normally obedient dog didn't come. He just sat there, staring at his master. "Kentucky, come here," Stone ordered firmly, but the dog ignored his command, turned, and walked away from him, disappearing behind the huge fallen log. Fearing the dog might be injured, Stone quickly dismounted and rushed toward the log as Kentucky pawed at the ground and began to whine.

Stone stooped to see what the dog had been digging at, and there, tucked into the rotted-out area of the fallen tree, he found his precious Juliette.

"Oh, Stone. I knew you'd come," she said in a mere whisper. "I've been asking God to send you."

"God led me to you, my beloved." As he squatted and leaned close to her, the sight that greeted him made his stomach lurch. He barely recognized his wife. A huge knot distorted her forehead, and she was covered with blood. He gently kissed her wounded face. "My darling, I've searched for you all night."

"I'm fi–fine," she whispered through chattering teeth, so softly he could barely hear her. "Th–thanks to Ke–Kentucky."

He tried to pull her from the log, but she winced in pain. "M—my a—arm. It—it's br—broken."

"Oh, Juliette, if it weren't for me—"

She gave a slight shake of her head. "No, d—don't s—say it," she whispered. "N—not your f—fault."

"I've got to get you to Doc Meeker. That nasty cut on your head and your broken arm both need attention." New energy filled his body as he tenderly scooped his wife from the log's crude opening, lifted her in his arms, and kissed her face. God had answered his prayers. He'd kept her safe. Even with her injuries, she was still the most beautiful woman he'd ever seen—far lovelier than Lucy had ever been.

Lifting his face to God, he called out loudly, "I praise You, God, for answering my prayers and leading me to my dear wife. Forgive me for ever doubting You!"

Turning to Kentucky, he asked, "Gonna make it, Boy?"

The big dog barked, then began ambling along behind them as they rode toward town to find Doc Meeker.

❧

"She'll be fine, Stone. Just make sure she gets plenty of rest. She's been through quite an ordeal," Doc said. "You take good care of her, you hear me?"

Stone nodded as he carefully gathered his wife up and lovingly placed her in the buggy John had brought for him to take Juliette home. "I will, Doc. She's precious to me."

Juliette's sound arm circled her husband's neck as he carried her up the steps and into their home.

"Da—da," Andrew called out in his baby voice as he reached his arms toward them.

"Looks like my son wants me," Stone said with a grin as he tenderly placed his wife on a chair and took the smiling child from America. "Look who I brought home, Andrew. It's your mama."

Eric reached out and touched the heavy layers of cloth that covered the knot on Juliette's forehead. "Does it hurt, Mama?" he asked with a look that tore at her heart.

She slipped an arm around the boy and pulled him close. "It's not as bad as it looks." Noticing Will staring at her, she reached out a hand.

The little boy came running to her and leaped onto her lap. "Ma-ma h–h–hut?"

Juliette bent and kissed the boy's sweet cheek. "Yes, Will. Mama hurt. But she's going to be all right, now that she's home with her three boys." She sent a loving glance toward Stone, who appeared to be trying to mask his tears.

Later that night over a cup of hot tea, Stone told Juliette how he'd prayed in the woods that morning and had asked God to forgive him for his sins and asked Him to save him.

"I'm so glad, Stone. We both needed to get our lives straightened out. God has been so patient with us. Neither one of us deserves His love."

Stone gazed into her lovely face. "I know." Then, he and Juliette held hands, bowed their heads, and thanked the Lord for keeping each of them safe and bringing them home to their family.

⁂

Two days later, after a nourishing supper of potato soup prepared by America, Stone put the boys to bed, then carried his wife into her room. He placed her on her bed and propped her up against a pile of pillows, then sat down beside her, took her free hand in his, and kissed her palm. "If you're up to it, we need to talk."

She gnawed at her lower lip. She'd been dreading this since the moment Stone had angrily stormed out of the house with the quilt under his arm. "Yes, we do."

He gazed into her eyes and blinked several times before speaking. "I need to apologize for my actions on Christmas Day."

She wanted to scream out, *Yes, you need to apologize! I did nothing to deserve your wrath. I only wanted to make you happy!* Instead, she kept her silence.

"I–I haven't been totally honest. When I was out there

looking for you and asking God to help me find you, I promised Him I would tell you everything. Even if you hated me for it. There's so much you don't know. I hardly know where to start." He gulped hard. "Maybe I'd better go back to the beginning."

She nodded, knowing as angry as his words might make her, she could never hate him. Nothing could make her hate him. She loved him too much.

"My father, and his father before him, owned huge tobacco plantations. We had a fine house and many servants. All of them were slaves, bought by my father and my grandfather. Even as a small child, I hated watching the slaves working so hard and being mistreated by my father. Although the other wealthy people of Kentucky thought of him as this fine, upstanding man, he wasn't! He was cruel. He used to get drunk and beat my mother. She never told anyone because of the shame she felt, but the slaves and I knew."

Juliette gasped as her hand rose to cover her mouth. "How awful!"

"I used to tell her of my big plans to leave and take her with me, but we both knew it'd never happen—not with my father being so rich and powerful. We'd never get away from him. When he'd beat her, I'd put cold cloths on her bruises, trying to make her feel better. She'd always smile and say it helped, but I doubted it did."

"Didn't your friends and neighbors see her bruises?"

"No, she'd stay in the house until they disappeared, cover them with powder, or make up stories about falling down our staircase. She never told anyone. No one would've believed her anyway. Many times, I heard my father tell his friends she drank heavily, but that wasn't true. She never took a drink. He said that as a cover-up for the way she looked, all bruised and sad."

"Oh, your poor mother. How awful it must've been for her. For both of you."

"Well, one night when I guess I was about sixteen, I found

my mother lying on the floor in her room in a pool of blood. My father was standing over her with a heavy candlestick in his hand. He'd been beating her with it. I grabbed it from his hand and hit him once. Real hard. On his head. He clutched his chest and fell across the bed. I didn't know what to do. My mother screamed for me to go get help, but I didn't. I just stood there, almost hoping he wouldn't make it."

Juliette let out a slight moan. "Oh, Stone."

"Moses went for help, but by the time someone arrived, Father was already dead. To protect me, Mother told them she'd hit him. But the doctor said the blow hadn't been enough to kill him. He'd died of a heart attack. Still, I knew better. I'd killed him. If I hadn't hit him, he wouldn't have had that spell with his heart. I'm sure of it."

"You were only sixteen at the time?"

"Yes. My mom and I did the best we could to run the place after my father died. She died about five years later—from her illness they said, but I always thought it was from a broken heart. As their only child, I inherited everything: the plantation, my father's business, his bank accounts—" He paused. "Everything. I freed all the slaves when my mother died, and I became the legal owner."

"That's when you freed Moses and America?"

He smiled. "Yes. Most of the slaves stayed with me. I improved their housing and gave them an honest wage for their labors. I ran that plantation until about nine years ago. That's when I decided to sell out and come west. I needed a change in my life, a new challenge."

"And America and Moses came with you?"

He shook his head. "Not at first. They stayed behind with the new owner. I brought the few possessions I wanted to keep with me to St. Louis. I made my home there for a year or so. I'd never planned to stay in Missouri. My sights were set on Kansas and the open prairie."

Juliette tilted her head. "What about Alice?"

"Alice? Oh, she's maybe my half-sister. Father just showed

up with her one day. He said he thought she might be his daughter and moved her in with us. We never knew her real mother's name, and Father wouldn't tell us. He said he'd been paying some woman to look after her since the day she was born. The woman had died, so he'd brought her home to us. That's another reason my mother died of a broken heart. If the truth were known, some of the slave children were probably my half-brothers and sisters too."

He sucked in a fresh breath of air and continued. "Alice is five years older than me. When she got old enough to be on her own, she left us and moved to St. Louis to get away from my father. That's one reason I stayed in Missouri—because of her. I'd always loved her, almost as much as if she'd been my real sister."

"Is that where you met Lucy? In St. Louis?"

He rubbed at his chin and stared at the wall as if seeing a vision of his deceased wife. "Yes. I met her at a dance one of my new friends took me to. She was beautiful—the prettiest and wildest girl I'd ever met. She took a shine to me too. I used to think she really liked me. Looking back, I sometimes wonder if she'd learned about the money I'd banked from the plantation's sale and only tolerated me because of it."

Juliette shifted her position with a frown as pain shot through her arm. "Stone, surely you don't mean that."

"I might've been wrong, but I guess I'll never know for sure. Anyway, I fell for that woman in a big way. She hung all over me. Kissing me and making over me like I was the catch of the century. No woman had ever done that before. In two weeks we were married. Just like that." He snapped his fingers.

"She must've really loved you, to marry you so quickly."

"Well, I know she spent my money like there was no bottom to the barrel. And she never wanted to move west, even though she knew from the beginning that'd been my plan. I promised her a fine house and servants. Finally, she agreed to give it a try. I came on ahead and bought the land and turned it into Carson Creek Ranch. After I built the house, I brought her here. Since I'd promised her servants, I wrote to America and asked if she and Moses would like to come to Kansas."

Juliette smiled. "Oh, but she had to have been pleased when she saw this fine house. She must've loved moving to Kansas, to the new frontier, and being with her husband again. I'm sure she missed you."

Stone let out a long, deep sigh. "No, she hated it. She complained about everything. The house wasn't formal enough for her. It was too isolated. Too hot. Too cold. Too far from a big city where the elegant parties were held. Nothing I did pleased her."

"But—you loved her," she inserted softly. "You've told me so, many times."

"I did love her—or I thought I did. I remembered watching the way my father treated my mother. I vowed then that I'd never marry a woman I didn't love. And when I did marry, it would be forever. I took my marriage vows seriously."

"I'm sure Lucy did too."

Andrew stirred in his bed.

"Let me nurse him. I'm sure he'll go right back to sleep," Juliette told him as she smoothed the covers beside her.

Stone bent over the crib and lifted the sleepy baby, placing him at his mother's side. "I'll go after a fresh cup of water while you nurse him."

❧

He moved to the other room and sat down in the chair beside the fireplace, cradling his head in his hands. *God, can You ever forgive me for deceiving Juliette? I don't want to hurt this wonderful woman anymore, but she has to know the truth. I need Your help. Give me the right words. I can't put this off any longer.* He rose, plunged the dipper into the pail of water, and filled her cup. *She's been through so much these past few days. Dare I heap any more on her?* With a heavy heart, he moved back into her room with the cup.

She smiled as he came through the door, motioning toward the sleeping baby, a trickle of milk still evident on his rosy little cheek. "Would you put him back in his bed, please?"

He nodded, took Andrew from her side, and carefully laid the sleeping baby in his crib.

As soon as he was seated again, Juliette reached out and cupped his chin with her hand. "Poor Stone, I never realized you'd been through so much."

With a heavy heart filled with guilt, he hung his head. "I don't want sympathy, Juliette. Please know I'm not telling all of this as an excuse for my behavior. I'm telling it because you deserve to know. What I've done is inexcusable."

She shook her head. "Nothing can be that bad. Go on. I'm listening."

He settled himself beside her and began again. "I even took Lucy back to St. Louis several times to purchase some of the fine items you've seen here." He grinned. "Some I didn't know you'd seen."

"I'm sorry. I never meant to—"

He put a finger to her lips. "You did nothing wrong. You only wanted to please me." He paused. "For awhile, she seemed happy. But she was soon as discontent as ever, saying her life with me here in Kansas bored her. She constantly threatened to leave me and find another man who would take her back to St. Louis. Then, she began to be sick around the clock, and Doc Meeker said she was with child. That news really upset her. She blamed me and said she'd never fit in her beautiful clothes again because of what I had done to her. She even talked about doing away with the baby."

Juliette gasped. "How could she?"

He shrugged and let out another deep sigh. Telling her all of this was harder than he'd ever expected, but he couldn't stop now.

"I finally talked her out of it. When Eric came into this world and she had a pretty rough delivery, she swore she'd never have another child."

"But she loved Eric, didn't she?"

"Maybe. When he wasn't crying or wet. Then America or I

had to take over. Lucy would go into hysterics, run into her room, and lock the door. She wouldn't come out until one of us had put him to sleep."

He stole a glance toward Andrew, sleeping peacefully in his bed, his stubby legs tucked up under his little bottom. "She never even considered nursing him. We lived like that for about three years, I guess. Those years were pretty miserable for both of us."

"But—I always thought you two were so happy! You worshipped that woman!"

"I misled you. My pride wouldn't let me reveal the truth. I don't know how one man could've been so stupid."

He continued. "To keep her from brooding, I took her to St. Joseph or Topeka several times a year to shop for the newest fashions. Sometimes, I think promising her those trips was all that kept our marriage together. She'd hug me, kiss me, and tell me how wonderful I was. Like an idiot, I believed her. When we were visiting in St. Louis, her friends would give grand parties. Lucy would pile curls on her head with those fancy ribbons, and she'd wear low-cut gowns that cost me a small fortune. She'd parade herself back and forth in front of all the men. They'd make over her and whisk her about the dance floor, while all the ladies watched and envied her and her beauty. She loved it."

"If she treated you so badly, why did you put up with it?"

He swallowed hard. He had to answer her question as honestly as he could, no matter how much it hurt him to verbalize the words. "Be–because I saw my father in me. I felt the same hatred and discontent that he felt for my mother. Oh, not for the same reasons. Lucy and my mother were nothing alike. But I knew I had the same power my father had. The same—"

"Same what?" she asked, her eyes wide.

He paused and nibbled at his lip. "The same anger. It scared me. I never wanted to see that anger unleashed. I kept it all buried inside me. I'd turn my back on the jealousy and the things that made me mad. I made myself believe the attentions those men paid her were really compliments for me because I'd been able to convince such a beautiful woman to become my wife. In truth, I deceived myself."

"But you had two children—"

"Oh, yes. That was the blow that nearly sent Lucy back to Kentucky. We had—" He bit his lip. *How can I say this?*

"I'm your wife, Stone. You can tell me anything," she whispered softly.

"We were together as husband and wife. Often. It was her way of controlling me. And, to be honest, I never complained."

Her cheeks flushed. "I–I think I understand. You needn't explain."

"Anyway, when Doc Meeker diagnosed her second pregnancy, again she turned on me. She was even more upset than the first time. She considered having the baby taken from her. Although she never admitted it, I'm sure she tried some home remedies her friends had told her about to get rid of the baby. I've always thought that's why Will was born deaf."

Her mouth sprang open. "How awful. I can't imagine any mother wanting to get rid of her baby!"

"I guess I'll never know. Anyway, she insisted I take her back to St. Joseph to have the baby. I got her a nice house, and I asked Alice to look in on her occasionally. I couldn't be gone from the ranch all the time."

"That's when she made the quilt squares?" Juliette asked, prodding gently.

He nodded. "Yes, she always loved doing needlework. She made those twelve blocks, or squares, or whatever you call them. But she never got them put together before she—"

"Before she died?"

"Patience, I'm coming to that. From that first minute when I took Will in my arms, I suspected something might be wrong with his hearing. His cry had a strange sound to it. He didn't sound anything like a normal baby. Lucy wouldn't even talk about it. She wanted to put him up for adoption as soon as possible, saying one child was enough. I wouldn't hear of it. We had terrible arguments. I'd never been so angry in my entire life, other than when my father was beating my mother."

Stone wished he didn't have to tell his whole sordid story, but she had to know. He looked at her beautiful face, now swollen from the bump on her head. If she hadn't been his wife, none of her injuries would have ever happened. He'd bear that guilt the rest of his life.

"Go on, please. I didn't mean to interrupt."

The lump in his throat nearly choked him. "She refused to come back to Dove City. She said she needed time to recuperate, so I hired a nurse for her and one to take care of the boys. She stayed on in St. Joseph while I came back to tend to the ranch. I got several of the men to take over for me and went right back."

"Many women have a hard time adjusting after giving birth. Perhaps she—"

"Actually, that's what I thought at first, but that had nothing to do with it. Will's birth—"

Her eyes widened. "That's when she died of childbirth complications? Like you'd told me?"

He clenched his fists and blinked. "No. I wish I could say she died from childbirth complications, but I can't. That was a lie!"

ten

A deep frown creased her forehead, and her face turned a ghostly white. "Wh–what do you mean?"

"She *didn't* die soon after Will was born. I lied."

"If she didn't die then, when did she die?" Juliette pressed herself tightly against the pillows, her face convulsing with anger. "Oh, Stone! Don't tell me she's still alive! If she is, that means you're still married!"

He reached out to her. "You've got it all wrong. Hear me out!"

She began to beat on him with her good hand. "How could you marry me, knowing your wife is still alive? How could you lie to me like that?"

He grabbed her wrist to fend off her blows. "She didn't die then! She died two years later!" She tried to pull away from him, but he held her fast, determined to tell her everything.

"But why? Why would you lie about such an important thing? It doesn't make any sense. Is anything you've told me the truth?"

"Everything I told you, up to the part about Lucy being upset about having a second baby and wanting to put Will up for adoption, is true."

"Go on."

"From that minute on, when she realized I was not going to agree to give him up, she said she hated me. Lucy actually told me she'd never loved me. It was my money and the lifestyle I could give her she was after. She called me names and refused to live under my roof any longer. I sent the children and their nurse over to my sister's house to stay. I hoped Lucy would feel differently about things once she got over having a second baby, but she didn't. She was moody and hateful. She'd attend parties at night, then sleep until noon the next day. She drank too heavily, and what time she wasn't sleeping or celebrating with her friends, she slept on the sofa with an empty bottle in her hand. Life was miserable for both of us. She constantly brought strange men to our house, and when I tried to send them away, she'd go with them."

Warily, he reached out and cupped her hand. "She'd be gone for days at a time. I had no idea where she was or who she was with. Then, one day, she walked in with this Mexican trader and announced she was tired of being married to me and living her dull, boring life. She was going to Mexico with him. Two hours later, she was gone, and so was a good bit of money from our bank account."

"I never knew. I thought the woman was a saint. I envied her."

"Juliette, I knew the day she walked out with that man, I'd never want her back. I'd rather live the rest of my life alone, raising our two sons by myself, than have her come back to me. She'd shattered every bit of pride I've ever had."

"Didn't you try to stop her?"

"I started to. She *was* my children's mother. I couldn't just let her walk out that way, without knowing how to reach her. I've told you about my anger. At times, I felt like strangling Lucy, I was so furious with her. I reminded myself of my father, and it made me sick. I was afraid if I got near the man, I'd kill him with my bare hands. Then my sons wouldn't have anyone to provide for them. I—I just stood there and watched them go."

"But the padlocked room? Her things? I don't understand."

"I'm getting to that." He turned her hand loose, rose, and began to pace about the room. After pulling his handkerchief from his pocket, he blew his nose loudly.

"I brooded around St. Joseph for awhile, but I knew I had to get back to my ranch. I couldn't ask my sister to leave her home and her friends, but I begged her to keep my boys until I could find someone here to care for them. She finally agreed. I was embarrassed and ashamed to admit my wife had walked out on me and my children. I think if it hadn't been for Eric and Will, I might have done away with myself. I didn't want anyone to know the truth, so when I finally came back to Dove City, I invented that lie and told everyone she'd died of complications after Will's birth—even though she was still alive. Since they had no reason to think otherwise, they believed me. I was consumed with guilt when people offered their sympathy. I've never told them any differently."

"What happened to Lucy? Did you ever hear from her again?"

He rubbed at his forehead. "No. Not a word—not even to ask about her children. But about two years later, almost to the day, on one my few trips to visit my sons, I ran into a friend of hers. She and Lucy had kept in contact with one another. She's the one who told me Lucy had died. Apparently, she came down with an illness in Mexico. She was sick for several months and eventually died. Her Mexican boyfriend had contacted the woman in St. Joseph and told her about Lucy's death. I tried to learn more for our sons' sake, but I was never even able to find out where she died or even the name of the man she left with."

She stared at him as if still trying to comprehend what he was saying. "Then why have you kept her things the way she left them?"

He sucked in another breath and let it out slowly. "I don't have an answer for that, Juliette. I guess because they remind me of happier times. Those first few months, I was captivated by her beauty and her charms. She was the kind of woman men dream about. I was stupid enough to believe she loved me. In truth, all she was doing was using me; but after Will was born and she didn't want him, my anger took over. The same uncontrolled anger I'd seen in my father. I wanted to smash everything she'd ever touched, get rid of everything that reminded me of her. I even wanted to burn the house down."

"I'm glad you didn't. It's the perfect place for your boys."

"My hatred consumed me. She never cared for me. I know

that now. It was my money she was after. For a year or so after she died, I kept that room locked and never opened it. I didn't want to touch her things or even see them. Because of her and what she'd done to me, I decided I'd never let a woman get close to me again. I refused to put myself in a position to be hurt again. All I wanted out of life was to bring my boys home."

Juliette wiped at her eyes. "I'm beginning to understand. It must have been a terrible time for you."

"The worst." He smiled at her. "Then I met you. You were from a fine family and seemed to be the perfect mother. I knew from the first day I met you, you were the woman I wanted to raise my boys. I also knew you were too proper to stay in my home and work for me unless I could talk you into marrying me. I brought you that handkerchief just to start up a conversation. I hoped eventually you'd agree, and I could bring my boys back where they belong."

"Then Mr. Stark was killed. Mrs. Stark decided to sell the hotel, and my father needed the money to buy it. Correct?"

"Yes. I'd have given anything to have my boys back home. I know it sounds like a devious plan, but honestly, Juliette, if you wouldn't have agreed to marry me, I would've given John the money."

She lowered her gaze and dabbed at her eyes again. "But you didn't have to, did you? You bought a wife instead."

"Yes," he conceded, "I bought a wife instead—a wife I never intended to love. I'd vowed I'd never love another woman. Not after the way I'd been hurt by Lucy. That's why I wanted a marriage in name only. I was never going to put myself in that position again. I only wanted a fine Christian woman to run my house and be a mother to my boys. I never planned on falling in love with you. Your father needed the money, and you wanted a home for you and your son." He paused, guilt ripping at him, tearing at his heart. "It seemed the best solution for all of us."

She began to weep uncontrollably. "All of us? For you, you

mean! The Baker family's needs were just a way for you to gain what you wanted. A business deal! We were just a means to an end. An end to your search for a way to bring Eric and Will to Dove City."

"I *was* concerned about your family!" he nearly shouted at her. Andrew stirred in his bed, and Stone lowered his voice before continuing. "I've never met a finer man than John. I would *never* have let that hotel get away from him. Even if I'd had to buy it and beg him to run it for me. But at that time, I had no idea *you'd* become so important to me!"

"Important to you? Is that what you call it?" She turned her face away as tears trailed down her cheeks and fell onto her gown. "What do you think all those people who've been calling you a hero would think if they knew you'd lied? Not only to me and my family, but to them? What do you suppose God thinks?"

"As their deputy, those folks trusted me. I'm sure they'd hate me for it." He shifted in the chair uncomfortably. "What does God think? He thinks I'm a fool," he answered softly, lowering his face into his hands.

"Please, leave," she said, her voice quivering. "Go into Lucy's room. Rock in her chair and remember the times she tossed you aside like an old boot!"

"But, Juliette—don't you see? I hated Lucy. That's why I went into that locked room night after night. I knew I was falling in love with you, and I didn't want to! By going in there and sitting in that chair, I reminded myself of the miserable life we'd had together. I had to convince myself taking you as a true wife might be no better than living with her." He hung his head, lacing his fingers together. "How did I know you wouldn't do the same thing to me that Lucy did if I told you I loved you? I've saddled you with a deaf child, just like I did her. How did I know you wouldn't try to take my money and leave me, just like she did?"

She glared at him, her eyes filled with anguish. "I thought you knew me better than that! You trusted me with your children!"

"I thought I knew her! Don't you see? I was afraid! Afraid of loving you! Afraid of losing you!" His voice softened again as he glanced toward the sleeping baby. "I thought I loved Lucy. But now, after being with you, I finally realize what I had with her was not true love. The love I had for Lucy was nothing like my love for you. In fact, if I were honest, I'd probably have to say what I had for her was lust, not love. I wanted to possess her. She was an object to hold up in front of people. There was constant strife between us, right from the beginning. We were never truly happy. Being with you, going on picnics, holding hands over the supper table, sitting on the floor in front of the fireplace, reading our Bible together, watching you with our boys, sitting beside you in church—that's true happiness—the kind of happiness God intended between a husband and a wife."

Juliette struggled to refute what he was saying, but no words came. She, too, had discovered true happiness by being with him.

"The love I have for you is different—sweet and sincere. Although you are a beautiful woman, I'm not interested in showing you off like an object I've purchased. I want you all to myself. I want to hold you, to shelter and protect you. I want to take you in my arms and shower your face with kisses. And yes, I want to take you to my bed, but only as a way to express my love for you. You're everything to me, Juliette. Can't you see that?"

He leaned his face close to hers, so close he could feel her warm breath on his cheeks. "Look into my eyes, Juliette. You're my wife. I'd lay down my life for you. Can't you see that? Can't you find it in your heart to forgive me?"

She gulped hard. "Th–this has all come as a shock, Stone. Ca–can we talk about this in the morning? I need time to think."

"Of course. But remember the things I've said. I love you, Juliette." With a look of defeat, he rose and slowly walked away.

❧

She spent a restless evening as the love she felt for Stone battled with the ill feelings she harbored in her heart for his deception. His lies had crushed her. She felt lower than she'd ever felt in her life. Yet, in some ways, her heart sang. He loved her. He really loved her. Wasn't this what she'd wanted all along?

Before she blew out the lamp, she pulled the Bible from her nightstand and held it to her bosom before turning the pages to the love chapter in First Corinthians. She read it silently, with an open heart. *Oh, God, I do love Stone. Help me! I want to make the right decision. What is Your will for our lives?*

Early the next morning she heard a slight rap on her door, and her heart began to pound furiously. "Juliette? Are you awake?" She quickly pulled the covers about her. "I—I guess so. Come in."

"I know you're furious with me. You have every right to be, but let me talk. I—I've been awake most of the night, reading my Bible and settling this thing with God. I asked for His forgiveness, and He has forgiven me. I know He has because it says so right in His Word. I've rid myself of the ghosts of my past. As soon as I can get to it, I'm going to take everything out of Lucy's room and give it all away. I know there are some things you'd like to have, but I'd rather buy them for you new than have them around as a reminder of her."

"Stone, I—"

"Shh, let me finish. I need to get these things said. I've wronged you, Juliette, and I've come to apologize." As he moved slowly to the bed and sat down beside her, she could see his eyes were puffy and he'd been crying. "I had no right to lie and deceive you like I did. There's no excuse for what I've done. I—I know I don't deserve it—but I hope, someday, you'll find it in your heart to forgive me. I—I never meant any harm, honest." A tear rolled slowly down his cheek.

"Come here. I have something to say too." She waited until

he'd seated himself, then continued. "When you told me you'd lied about Lucy's death, I–I felt completely devastated. If it hadn't been for Eric and little Will, I would have taken Andrew and gone back to the hotel. But—" She paused, wanting to say just the right words to convey her sincere feelings. "I spent a long time with my Bible last night. God has been speaking to my heart too. About forgiveness. I–I love your precious boys. While I can't condone all the lying you've done, I can almost see why you did. Experiences that shake our lives and turn them upside down can make us respond in strange ways. I still intend to stay true to my wedding vows. When I made those vows, I made them before God. I feel He would have me stay." Her heart clenched as a slow smile crept across his face.

"You mean it? You'll stay?"

"We're both sinners saved by grace, Stone, and we're still legally married. I'll stay if you want me to. I–I love you too."

"You do? You really do?" His hand lightly touched hers. "I love you more than life itself."

She felt his fingers tighten over hers.

"With God's help, do you think we can work this out? That you can find it in your heart to forgive me for lying to you? I love you so much, my dearest. God has forgiven me. Do you think you'll ever be able to forgive me?"

She gazed into his eyes, his words of repentance softening the ache in her heart. "I'd strayed away from Him too. I'd been playing at church. Through all of this, I've discovered I need a closer walk with Him. God has forgiven me, so I must forgive you."

"I'll never lie to you again. I promise I'll do everything in my power to restore your faith in me. I want God to control our lives and be the Head of our household."

She reached out and touched his cheek as Andrew stirred in his crib. "I love you, Stone. I think I've always loved you. I was just afraid to admit it. I want to be your wife in every way."

epilogue

Juliette's arms circled her husband's neck as she gazed into his kind face with adoring eyes. "Do you realize this will be our fourth Christmas together?"

"Sure do." He gave her a broad grin, then nestled his chin in her hair. "I've loved every day of our time together."

"Stone," she began slowly, smoothing back the hair from his forehead, knowing her words might upset him. "I've been thinking about that quilt."

The smile on his face disappeared.

"It's a beautiful quilt. It seems a shame to have it boxed away, out of sight. I think it's time we did something with it."

He frowned. "Like what?"

"I put in many nights of work on that quilt. Probably far more than I should have. I wanted it to be a special gift for you. If you agree, I'd like to remove Lucy's name from those blocks and embroider my own name in those places. After all, I'm the one who put it together, bound it, and did all the hand quilting."

He tilted her chin upward and gazed into her eyes. "You sure you want to do that?"

She stood on tiptoes and kissed his cheek. "Yes, my love, I do. I've forgiven you for what you did to me, and I think it's time we both forgave Lucy, don't you?"

"You're quite a woman, Juliette, and you're right. How could I have expected God to forgive me when I haven't been willing to forgive Lucy?" Stone wrapped his long arms about her waist and pulled her close. "Of course, it's all right with me. Anything to make you happy. But—are you sure having that quilt around won't bring back too many unpleasant memories? Perhaps it'd be better if we just gave it away."

"We're so happy together now. Our boys are growing up. Will is able to communicate with us. My mother's health has improved, and the hotel is doing well. God has blessed us in so many ways. With His help, I'm sure we can put all those bad memories aside. I'd rather think of the joy I felt as I labored on that quilt. Each stitch I added, I added with love for you, my darling. In many ways, our life together is wrapped up in that quilt."

"God has been good to us, hasn't He?"

She nodded. "Far more than we deserve."

"I love you, Juliette Piper."

"I love you too, dear Stone."

"You're truly a gift from God. If you want the quilt, it's fine with me. Now I realize how much work you'd put into it. I only wish I'd appreciated it at the time. I was a fool to react the way I did when you gave it to me. An utter fool!"

Juliette planted a kiss on her husband's cheek. "Shh, remember? Those bad memories are behind us now." She could feel his loving gaze upon her as she moved to the closet and pulled a box from the top shelf. Her fingers trembled as she removed the lid and lifted out Lucy's quilt.

A Letter To Our Readers

Dear Reader:

In order that we might better contribute to your reading enjoyment, we would appreciate your taking a few minutes to respond to the following questions. We welcome your comments and read each form and letter we receive. When completed, please return to the following:

Rebecca Germany, Fiction Editor
Heartsong Presents
PO Box 719
Uhrichsville, Ohio 44683

1. Did you enjoy reading *Lucy's Quilt* by Joyce Livingston?
   ❑ Very much! I would like to see more books by this author!
   ❑ Moderately. I would have enjoyed it more if

   _____

   _____

   _____

2. Are you a member of **Heartsong Presents**? ❑ Yes ❑ No
   If no, where did you purchase this book? _____

   _____

3. How would you rate, on a scale from 1 (poor) to 5 (superior), the cover design? _____

4. On a scale from 1 (poor) to 10 (superior), please rate the following elements.

   ____ Heroine   ____ Plot
   ____ Hero   ____ Inspirational theme
   ____ Setting   ____ Secondary characters

6. How has this book inspired your life?_____
_____
_____

7. What settings would you like to see covered in future
   Heartsong Presents books? _____
   _____
   _____

8. What are some inspirational themes you would like to see
   treated in future books? _____
   _____
   _____

9. Would you be interested in reading other **Heartsong
   Presents** titles? ❑ Yes   ❑ No

10. Please check your age range:
     ❑ Under 18   ❑ 18-24
     ❑ 25-34   ❑ 35-45
     ❑ 46-55   ❑ Over 55

Name_____
Occupation _____
Address _____
City_____ State_____ Zip_____
E-mail_____

Prairie County Fair

In Prairie Center, Kansas, all of Prairie County gathers *After the Harvest* for its first organized fair, and Judith Timmons hopes it's the last event she has to attend before moving back East.

As Anita Gaines prepares entries for the 1905 fair, she also faces *A Test of Faith*. Will she find the love of her life only to lose him?

Garrison Gaines enters Prairie Center society as a judge at the 1946 fair cook-off. Will he find a *Goodie Goodie* there to benefit his new catering business?

At the fair's "beautiful baby" contest rehearsals, old high school friends Zachary Gaines and Beth Whitrock renew acquaintances. Can a man who has vowed never to marry again have *A Change of Heart*?

Historical, paperback, 336 pages, 5 ³⁄₁₆" x 8"

❤ ❤ ❤ ❤ ❤ ❤ ❤ ❤ ❤ ❤ ❤ ❤ ❤ ❤ ❤ ❤ ❤ ❤ ❤

❤ ❤ ❤ ❤ ❤ ❤ ❤ ❤ ❤ ❤ ❤ ❤ ❤ ❤ ❤ ❤ ❤ ❤

Hearts❤ng

Presents

Great Inspirational Romance at a Great Price!

Heartsong Presents books are inspirational romances in contemporary and historical settings, designed to give you an enjoyable, spirit-lifting reading experience. You can choose wonderfully written titles from some of today's best authors like Peggy Darty, Sally Laity, Tracie Peterson, Colleen L. Reece, Debra White Smith, and many others.

When ordering quantities less than twelve, above titles are $3.25 each.
Not all titles may be available at time of order.

ℋEARTSONG ♥ PRESENTS

Love Stories Are Rated G!

That's for godly, gratifying, and of course, great! If you love a thrilling love story but don't appreciate the sordidness of some popular paperback romances, **Heartsong Presents** is for you. In fact, **Heartsong Presents** is the only inspirational romance book club featuring love stories where Christian faith is the primary ingredient in a marriage relationship.

Sign up today to receive your first set of four, never-before-published Christian romances. Send no money now; you will receive a bill with the first shipment. You may cancel at any time without obligation, and if you aren't completely satisfied with any selection, you may return the books for an immediate refund!

Imagine. . .four new romances every four weeks—two historical, two contemporary—with men and women like you who long to meet the one God has chosen as the love of their lives. . .all for the low price of $10.99 postpaid.

To join, simply complete the coupon below and mail to the address provided. **Heartsong Presents** romances are rated G for another reason: They'll arrive Godspeed!

YES! Sign me up for Hearts♥ng!